Char Broiled

SIG SAUER

Renko Styranka

The characters and events within Char Broiled are fictional, and any resemblance to persons and events, real or imagined, is coincidental.

Published by Xyster Multi Media Art
Xystermma.com
E-mail: Xystermma@gmail.com

Cover art: New Westminster Dusk, by Kelly Ulrich

ISBN: 0986967203
ISBN-13: 9780986967207

To fallen soldiers and their families.
Ten percent of the author's royalties will be donated
to various charities benefiting these heroes.

1

The intrusive vision that inhabited my mind after waking was always the same and, frame by frame, as it had been for real: the enrobed Afghan man standing above the dead child, a long, blood-stained falchion in one hand, his erection in the other. This incident had transferred a rage that would never in my life abate. I shot for the face. There was more satisfaction in it and no chance for them. Five lay dead, including the rapist. They had probably all raped the child. When I rose from bed, I witnessed again the scene in a kind of opaqueness that overlaid the supposed real world and could actually feel in my palms the steamy heat of the gun barrel and smell the gun smoke as it wafted in the baked clay room, mingling with the stench of blood and semen.

As usual, I woke too early. On my second to last day of my final tour, I had rolled in an armored vehicle and suffered third degree burns over 40 percent of my body below the neck. The pain in the skin on my chest and back had become intolerable, like salt and sandpaper in an open wound. I had suffered two years of it, the option of suicide my only companion, till I met Doctor Sylvain.

I found the remote and activated the spinal implant, a neurotransmitter. Slight vibrations overtook me. In a few moments, the incessant pain would be masked, and I could make it through another day. Severe nausea and fear swept over me though, a remnant of the days where there was no hope for it.

I stood in my bathroom facing the mirror, my cheeks lathered in Barbasol Beard Buster, the medicinal odor anything but soothing. The wall clock in the living room ticked softly, which for most people is a quieting sound. To me it is a time bomb.

I stared at my face for a moment and observed the ambiguous Japanese/German lines that my heritage had drawn, the life and personality that had colored the sketch. If I grew my hair long, the police thought I was native. If I highlighted it, people thought I was from Hong Kong. I could pass for Spanish, Venezuelan, or Thai. It was part of the gift.

After I shaved, I went into the living room and stood with an earthen mug of coffee and stared out the window over the railway tracks, to the Fraser flowing swiftly, deadly eddies forming and dissolving flow, the steely grey water churning hemlock deadheads like they were toothpicks.

I made my way back to the kitchen table and took up *The Sun* and reread the article:

Three Men Shot Dead
Vancouver: Three men were found shot dead in a Surrey apartment Monday morning. All were members of the Red-Legged Tarantulas,

a gang of predominantly Oriental men. According to an electrician who discovered the bodies, all three had been shot once in the face. None of the victims' names have been released at this time.

"It appears the war is escalating," RCMP spokeswoman Angie Cowell said. "As the flow of drugs increased from Mexico, we had expected a reduction of violence. This is definitely a setback for us."

A week earlier two members of the MP (Melting Pot) gang were gunned down in the parking lot of the River Rock Casino. No witnesses have come forward in either of the killings. Vancouver's Integrated Homicide Investigation Team, IHIT, had no more comment at this time.

I went to my bedroom and put on a pair of jeans, found a green and orange windowpane patterned shirt, and picked up my black, bulletproof Miguel Caballero leather jacket and checked the pockets for my wallet and keys. I tossed the shirt and jacket onto the bed just as there came a loud rapping on my door. I went to get it.

Standing outside in the hall were two CSIS agents. The one on the right was middle-aged, with matted brown hair and a moustache. He had on blue slacks and a brown sport jacket over a blue golf shirt. His name was Wil Mahood. The man on the left was a serious A-type redneck muscle head with short-cropped, bristly hair and a round, puffy face borne of years of steroid abuse. His name was Jake O'Malley.

"Haven't seen you at the office, Char," Jake said. "What's up?"

There was no smile on his face. His eyes peered past me into my condo.

I let them in and closed the door behind them. We went into the kitchen. Jake stood near the window after snooping a bit, his eyes glancing in the direction of the bedroom.

"That coffee I smell?" Wil asked.

"Yup."

Jake O'Malley's eyes roamed the whole of my torso.

"Jesus Christ, man. That happen in Afghanistan?"

"What do you guys want?" I asked.

"You're supposed to report in. We need to know you're all right," Wil said.

At first glance, Mahood looked like a high school principal, but his friendly demeanor belied his eyes, which resembled shards of ice chipped from a thousand-year-old ice shelf.

"If someone flips my switch, it's flipped. Nothing you can do after the fact."

They chewed on that. O'Malley stared at me for a second and then averted his eyes.

Mahood said, "You lift weights in your sleep? You're like a two-hundred-pound Bruce Lee."

My condition had not precluded my workouts, one of the few things I had left.

"If you hate the life so much," O'Malley said, while looking out the window at the river, "why'd you get into it in the first place?"

"Drinking doesn't work," I told him flatly. I went to the bedroom to get my shirt and jacket and said as I went, "Help yourself to some java if you want."

I put on the shirt and tucked it in, shrugged into the Caballero, and went back out into the main living area. Both agents had a coffee cup in their hands and sat, O'Malley on the brown leather sofa and Mahood on the matching loveseat.

"Don't run out on us," Mahood said. "We haven't had a chance to talk. Don't lose sight of the target."

"That's the problem with people today," I said to them. "No patience. Cell phones, e-mail, downloads…everyone wants it now. Undercover work takes time. You have to build trust before you can use it like a nail at the end of a two-by-four."

"Don't get too caught up in the life," O'Malley said. "Before you know it…"

"You don't take 'roids to build brainpower," I said.

"Take it easy, Sadao," Mahood said. He stood and stepped forward between me and O'Malley. "We just stopped by to make sure you're okay. You're two days late on reporting in."

These two were automatons. Their bosses wound them up first thing in the morning before marching them out the door.

"Next time call," I said.

My eyes found the window. Outside, on the railway tracks, a homeless man dressed in a long, tattered discolored overcoat struggled with a shopping cart piled with crap and corruption, bouncing it over the ties.

"You guys done with your coffee? I have things to be and places to do."

They left as quickly as they had come, the Irishman avoiding my eyes. I waited ten minutes to leave so that if anyone was watching they wouldn't see us together. I turned on the alarm, activating the pinhole camera, and went the fuck out into a sunny day most people would have deemed agreeable.

2

This contract had begun the way most things had in my life—pure chance. A former commander, Chuck Zbintov, who was good friends with a CSIS chief named Antoine L'Ouiseau, had recommended me. L'Ouiseau sounds like bird in French. Most guys with names like that get nicknames like Swallow or Budgie. Antoine was called Vulture, but only behind his back, the way no one ever called Bugsy Segal Bugsy to his face. Tough nicknames are earned, says Char.

I didn't meet with Vulture at CSIS offices, but was flown to Montreal and driven in a Lincoln Town Car by a battered, grizzled Frenchman to a mansion in Westmount. The home was built of massive granite blocks and seemed colder than the snow blanket on the three acres surrounding it. When I stepped from the Town Car, it was so cold outside my breath hung in the air like a haunting spirit. The car drove off without the chauffer muttering a word.

The arcing walk was shovelled but glazed and slippery nonetheless. All the windows in the huge home were lit and glowing, and there looked to be about seventy-five of them. I approached the eight foot, peaked wooden door that looked like it belonged on Castle Rhone, and just as I was about to ring the bell, the thing creaked open. I stepped through and in from the cold.

An aged butler faced me. His frame was blockish, and his suit hung loosely as it would have if it had been draped over an upright casket. His jaw was a busted parallelogram that looked as though it could chomp down on a truck axle while he bent it in two with his thick, meaty paws.

"Your jacket, sir," he said, taking my Caballero, scarf, and gloves from me. His slight accent was Eastern Bloc, Polish perhaps. "This way, Mr. Sadao."

He had huge thighs and needed to swing his legs wide to walk.

The air inside the mansion was warm enough, but the house was dark and austere, to say the least. My eyes strained to see my way through, as if in a black fog. Unease crept through me like spiders in my veins.

I passed a fabulous oil painting of fish underwater, swashes of gold and yellow and orange pushing out into the hallway. There was a suit of armor in a corner of the hall, and I didn't doubt it was authentic. It had a large dent in the side of the breastplate and on the top of the helmet. We entered a library lined with bookshelves twelve feet high, and at the far end, there was a fireplace you could have driven a Yaris into, in which burned a good chunk of tree. A tufted oxblood leather sofa and two matching chairs angled to face the fire. In one of the chairs sat a silhouette of a man.

The butler introduced us. "Mr. L'Ouiseau, Mr. Sadao to see you sir."

"Thank you, Pavel."

The Vulture stood to greet me and shook my hand. His eyes assessed me objectively but politely. With a wave, he offered me a seat facing him and then sat himself.

"Would you like a drink?" Vulture asked.

"I thought you'd never ask. Bourbon if you have it."

Vulture picked up a phone next to him, dialled five, and said to it, "Bring Mr. Sadao a Woodford," then set the thing down and rubbed his hands up and down his thighs.

He had on a beautiful two-tone blue smoking jacket, even though he wasn't smoking, and looked younger than I had expected, fifty perhaps. He was a thin man with angular, handsome features and jet-black hair that sparkled against the firelight. Though he stared at the flames, his eyes reflected none of it. I looked into the fire and let myself be hypnotized by it till Pavel came with my drink, a full four ounces in an exquisite highball glass etched with crossed swords. I wondered if the swords meant anything, like membership into a club.

I took the glass, swirled the brassy liquid, and took a swig. It tasted sweet, like cherries. I held it up between me and the fire and said, "Priming me with copious amounts of quality liquor, I see."

"Anything to grease the slide," he said, chuckling. It was not a happy laugh and sounded more in tune with the crackling of the fire, like how Satan himself might laugh.

"I've been in worse spots. I can guarantee that," I said, taking a long pull on the bourbon.

This drew a smile from Vulture. As I looked at the outline of his face in the gloom, he rather looked like a carrion. Perhaps that was where he'd gotten his name. Perhaps he got it from putting his face in the entrails. I'd have that in common with him at least.

"Well, Char, we'll see about that." He drew in a breath and continued talking while ignoring the drink in his left hand. "You come highly recommended, but then so have many others. If I can't find my leading man, I won't make the picture. Simple as that. Here's the deal: I need a name. The way you're going to get that name is by infiltrating gang culture in your hometown. You'll become a mole. You actually work well for us, here. You've come back from Afghanistan, struggled with health and assimilation. You have no work or even any prospects. You're cover is that you fall into the life out of necessity. How you portray that is up to you. No connection to local police. You'll have a get-out-of-jail-free card, but don't be stupid enough to act like you do. You…"

"Who am I looking for?" I asked.

"We don't know," he said forlornly. "That's what we need you to find out."

"I'm lost," I said.

"B.C. bud is a six billion dollar a year industry. Most of it leaves via the Vancouver port, which is run by the Lone Wolves. What's coming back is heroine, ecstasy, humans, and weapons, not necessarily to Vancouver or Canada, but in reciprocation to the bud. We want to find out who and what is on the other end of a new supply, coming from Asia we think. We haven't been able to even come close. Normal surveillance doesn't work in situations like this. The Lone Wolves and gangs in general have a sophisticated hierarchy. You have to run the gauntlet to get anywhere with them. The problem…"

"I have an idea," I said, interrupting him.

He stopped midsentence, his mouth hanging on an unsaid syllable, and then said, "You have an idea? What idea?"

"You don't have to be a rocket sergeant, Mr. L'Ouiseau. You want dope on the dope coming in. I have an idea how to get in. What's in it for me?"

The fire crackled and began to burn more furiously, creating strange licks on the stone walls and mahogany bookcases.

Vulture grinned and sipped at last from his glass, sighed reflectively, and said, "What's in it for you? Well, let's see. You have no job, no direction. Your former commander tells me you couldn't hold a straight job now if your life depended on it, which it may. Chuck has great respect for you, I must say. So, what you get is a high-paying job you can actually do."

"How high paying?"

"Ten grand a month plus expenses. Free car of your choice. One million tax free if you get us the name and pinpoint him."

I nearly dropped my glass. Had it not held Woodford Reserve, I might have.

"Taxpayers can afford this?"

"The RCMP and Crown often pay witnesses much more than that, Mr. Sadao. This job may consume your life for the next several years and may provide the final nails in your coffin. It could also set you up for life. But consider it a favor to Canada and our mutual friend."

I felt none of the patriotism one might have thought. Vulture was right, though. I had no future, no prospects, nothing. In life, there are forks in the road that inevitably alter you forever.

"As a sidebar," Vulture said, "IHIT is confounded by some murders in their jurisdiction, maybe gangland, maybe not. Not even IDs on the victims yet. Eyes peeled."

I felt my chest swell with a rush of adrenaline. I reached for the remote clipped to my belt and upped the ante.

"I hear you can really scrap,"Vulture said as we polished off the whiskey. "You into the UFC?"

"I've been to several events live," I said, "but as the Gracies say, it's different than fighting in an alley. Or with guns. It's one thing to train for a fight in a cage, on a mat, with a ref, another thing entirely to fight for your life in a biker bar or battlefield, a hundred unplanned variables putting their boot up your arse. But the UFC is the purest sport we have."

Vulture nodded knowingly. Tapping his temple he said, "Winning is 80 percent mental."

3

The Lone Wolves were top dog, so to speak. From them shit flowed downhill. My idea was this: pick a Lone Wolves patch member to rescue. Everybody likes to be rescued, and everybody is grateful to his rescuer. I wouldn't mention I'd be the reason he'd need saving.

When I got back to Vancouver, I transferred the disc file Vulture had given me to a netbook I'd purchased for the case. In the file were lists of gangs and their members, affiliates, associates as well as addresses of clubhouses and businesses owned by the gangs. I decided off the bat to keep copious records. I'd never remember everything I'd need to know.

The Lone Wolves had twenty-five full-patch members, and eighty-five strikers and associates, not counting the mid- and lower-level gangs that essentially worked for them. Vincent Knight was their president. Marc Glasner and Marty Smuker were his heavy hitters, his goons, bodyguards, fixers, cleaners, and never far away from Knight. Marty seemed like the more interesting of the two.

According to the file, Smuker stood 6'3" and tipped the Toledo at 325. From the photos, he seemed to carry a little extra around the midsection and could be defined with what, in an unfortunate turn of phrase, is referred to as hard fat. The mug shot showed an Hispanic face covered with tiny, pale scars, which was congruous to his ten years in and out of juvenile facilities and prisons. His broad nose had been properly flattened for good. His arms were sleeved in badly wrought prison tattoos, his back emblazoned with the Lone Wolves crest.

The man could be summed up by this story: Before he was a biker, when he was just twenty-two, he had parlayed his income from a finely tuned B&E operation into a black, flamed 1970 Nova muscle car and had entered it in a hot rod show in Kelowna. Legions of bikers were in town, on their way to a jamboree somewhere in Washington State. Two patched Outlaws came by his display. One made the mistake of spitting on the hood of Marty's car. Ten minutes later, paramedics were carting the Outlaws away, one convulsing, and police were cuffing Smuker and putting him into the back of a cruiser.

A witness who wished to remain anonymous said that he had never seen a man move so quickly, no matter the size. Smuker had leapt at the first Outlaw, a man Smuker's size, and popped him with a right to the chin, knocking him senseless. The second Outlaw, several inches taller than Smuker but lanky and gawky, ducked and weaved and popped Smuker before hoofing him with his square-toed engineering boots, to no affect whatsoever. Smuker got hold of the Outlaw and rag-dolled him while dismantling his face with elbows, then dropped him to the ground, tore a piece off the biker's shirt to wipe off the spittle from the hood of the Nova, and nonchalantly went for the Mother's car polish.

I thought carefully about my plan. I couldn't use anyone from Vancouver: it was too dangerous. The three men I called in for this job ran a dojo in Toronto where I had trained. A significant portion of their income came from choreographing fight scenes in movies, but these weren't ballerinas—these were fighters down to their shoelaces.

I followed Smuker for a month before deciding the best place to get him was not outside one of the bars he frequented or on one of his money-collecting jaunts, when someone might come to his aid, but in a downtown parking lot he parked in every Tuesday evening while visiting a call girl who lived in a townhouse south of Robson. The parking lot was perfect. It was small, dark, and not someplace anyone would go to break up a fight.

"Hit him with the pipe first," I told Jasminder.

Jas stood six feet tall and weighed a solid 195. He had long, stringy black hair and pale, patchy skin. He looked gothic rather than East Indian.

"You got it, man," he said calmly.

The men he picked to come with him were larger than Jas, in the mid-230s. Stan had a goatee and shaved head. Jimbo's round baby face was clean shaven, and on his head, he wore a black skull cap. All three wore dark clothing. We went over the details one last time and put our cell phones on vibrate and took our positions.

Marty's orange 2009 Challenger was nosed in against the hedge running along the sidewalk. I looked at my Torch for the time.

Marty came up the street right at ten thirty, with the sky completely blackened, but he was carrying a paper grocery bag and walking with an old woman on the opposite side of the street. It was a warm day in late spring, with no wind and only the muffled sounds of downtown echoing through the alley. I phoned my men and cued them and told them Marty may approach his car from a slightly different angle than we had planned.

Marty went with the old woman to the foyer of her building, which was directly across the street from the parking lot and hedge. When she opened the door, he set the bag in her arms and watched her as she made her way to the elevator.

"Not even Edwin Alonzo Boyd was all bad," I said aloud.

A powerful waft of marijuana smoke enveloped me. I looked around but couldn't see anyone else in the alley.

Marty left the building and came straight across the street and went through a hedge to get to his car.

I stepped blindly forward through the dark alleyway, but as I approached the parking lot, the light got better. I heard scuffling and picked up the pace.

I heard a ping sound ring out and a loud, "What the? Jeezuz!"

I saw Marty drop and then pop back up again. The fucker could move. He was light even on the balls of one foot.

I let my men go at him for a few seconds, silent in their work. We'd discussed dialogue, but Marty wouldn't be surprised someone was attacking, unless he was expecting a simple, sure-fire bullet.

"Just kick the shit out of him," I'd decided, "but don't KO him. I need him to see me breaking it up."

Marty was backed against his car, unable to move forward or sideways on his broken leg. Jimbo hit him with a terrific shot to the mandible that would have put a lesser man down.

"State your case, man," Marty Smuker told them through bloody lips. His face was already puffy. He touched his fingertips to his wound and looked at the blood. The three had been lucky they'd hit Smuker first with the pipe.

I bull-rushed the three men from the side, knocking Stan and Jimbo to the ground, and then took a swing at Jas, aiming for his forehead.

"Now it's three on two," I said.

"It's none of your fucking business," Jas said excitedly. "Stay the fuck out of this."

Stan and Jimbo were up now and came in at me, and I hit Jas high with a roundhouse kick, something we'd planned. He went down.

I could sense Marty looking at me, staring a hole through the side of my head.

"This ain't over, fat man," Jas said to Marty. Jas looked around frantically, feigning worry that police might show up. "Next time you won't be so lucky. I'm gonna feed your balls to you."

Jas and his men did a stellar job of acting harried and agitated. They got out of there as fast as they could, before anyone else came on the scene, like a cruiser.

"You okay man?" I asked Marty, pretending to give a shit.

Smuker eyed me warily at first and said, "They broke my fucking leg with the pipe. I'd have fist-fucked 'em if they hadn't broken my leg."

I didn't doubt him.

"St. Paul's is just down the road. Let me drive you there," I said.

He nodded, his face beaded with sweat. He was going into shock. His femur was broken, worse than I had thought. If you break your leg bad enough, you can sever the femoral artery and bleed to death inside your own leg. It'd be hard to detect swelling on this man.

"Take me in my car," he said. He fumbled the keys into my palm and shuffled on one leg to the passenger side. He opened the door and adjusted the seat all the way back to allow his frame entry, grunting in agony and short of breath.

I got in and started the engine. The car was fully loaded and had a nitrous oxide switch. The hemi rumbled and whined as I backed it up and put it in first gear. Trip hop blasted out of the stereo, but Marty angrily turned it off. He rode silently, in great pain, leaning back with his eyes closed, sucking wind every so often.

I pulled the car to the emergency room door and got out and helped him inside, where he tried sitting in a wheelchair but fell over, toppling the chair with him. A nurse behind the front desk saw us and hurried over.

"He broke his leg," I told her, "the femur. It looks bad."

"All right," she said. "I'll get help."

She left me standing there and Marty on the floor turning as white as a beluga.

"Thanks, man," Marty managed to say.

"Is there someone I can call for you?" I asked, again feigning concern.

He looked at me as if I was crazy.

Yeah, Marty, no one gives a shit about you, me included.

"Look, I'll wait for you, drive you home."

"Why are you doing this?" he asked.

"Hey, man, no one's ever helped me when I've been down," I lied.

The nurse came back with two burly orderlies, and as they struggled to get Marty on a gurney, the big man stretched his arm out to shake my hand.

Phase one of operation sucker punch: complete.

4

I went to the underground where I kept the 2006 Nissan Skyline GT-R I'd purchased from an auto broker specifically for this job. I wanted to give off a balls-to-the-wall image. It had been converted from right- to left-hand drive and sprayed to look like polished aluminum, with a whale tail on the boot lid that popped up and down with the flip of a toggle. It had been through a California tuner where the engine and suspension had been pimped. All wheel drive transferred 785 hp to asphalt. It only had 7.000 kilometers on the odometer. I was an oriental-looking man in Vancouver, and this Japanese supercar gave the right impression. Nice cars blend in here.

I checked the carpet I'd affixed to the cement pillars on either side of my stall, which were intact and kept me from scrapping the paint. Several other tenants had gotten the idea and had aped me. The entire garage had pillars covered in bits of carpet.

I stepped in the car and breathed in the still new-leather odor, started the engine, and listened to the high roar as I revved it and checked the tach. My favorite thing about the car was that the speedometer went to four hundred klicks. I headed out of the parking garage and onto Front Street.

It pissed me off that the CSIS agents, O'Malley and Mahood, had been directed to stop by and check up on me, but nobody trusts anybody in that biz. They weren't worried about my health; they wanted me to know they were watching, so I wouldn't fall to temptation. I made a mental note to call straight to the man, Vulture, and get that horseshit halted.

I ran a few errands and stopped to have the car detailed and then headed to Surrey, to a rural property owned by Marty, east of 176th off Eighty-eighth. Now that the weather was turning for the better, he was having a little shindig on his newly constructed back deck and wanted me to come by, to show his thanks for helping him with his broken leg.

An ancient, rotted dugout canoe that looked authentic Haida marked the driveway. The entire section of land was surrounded by cedar hedges and, behind that, chain link fence. The road twisted so you couldn't see onto the property till you were in it. It was what you'd have expected.

A huge monstrosity of a house rose from the field like a pimple on the tip of Heidi Klum's nose. I'll never understand why people in the northwest cover houses with stucco. No matter how you paint it, it gets moldy and begins to take on a sickly hue, like day-old cat vomit. The home looked nice otherwise, with tall, wide windows, a flat stone entry, a massive chimney, and fine cedar trim around the windows. Off to the side was a three car garage and in front of that a row of custom Harley choppers glimmering in the afternoon sunlight. A yellow Hummer, Marty's Challenger, and a blue Land Rover were parked there as well. A piece of wet plywood, a rusted bicycle, a deflated soccer ball, a dilapidated swing set, and other forgotten items were strewn across the patchy lawn surrounding the house. The impression was that even though there was a lot of money about, it was slowly sinking into the mud.

I parked away from the others and got out and checked myself in the window of the Skyline. I adjusted the collar of my shirt under the Caballero, shrugged myself comfortable, and regarded my face in the glass. No acting required. The last two years of my life had given me the look of someone who'd just as soon bite off your fucking head as talk to you. I put my hands in the pockets of my leather and walked around back, where I heard all the music and jabber.

If my tours of Afghanistan had taught me anything, it was kinesics. Understanding the body language of whatever tribe you're interacting with was crucial to success. While walking toward the stairs up to the deck where everyone gathered, I noticed that all the men faced each other square. Fighting is done at angles, so perhaps that was a tactic to not look aggressive. There were some women here, but they were greatly outnumbered. As I went up the stairs, a long-bearded, long-haired man ordered a plump, middle-aged woman with a cigarette stuck to her bottom lip to get him another beer, even though the cooler was right behind him.

Don't show women respect around these dudes, I thought.

I didn't see Marty right away and didn't want to appear out of place or uncomfortable. I acted like I belonged there by going straight for the cooler and digging from the ice a Sleeman's and screwed off the cap.

The bearded man was no more that ten feet away and staring straight at me, his beer held at his hip. He wore a silver chain and on that a three-inch bear claw pendant with mother-of-pearl inlays on the sliver mount. He saw me looking at it and fingered it.

"Grizzly claw," he said, his voice gruff like Tom Waits's. He let go of the pendant and extended his bent and twisted hand. "Vincent," he said. "You must be Char."

I hadn't recognized him at first. The mug shot I'd seen was of a younger man, head shaved and chest covered in tattoos. This man was Vincent Knight, club president of the Lone Wolves.

I shook his hand and withstood his eyes roving over me. He had on Western boots and had three or four inches on me, but most of his bulk was flab and man boobs.

A woman behind him momentarily caught my eye. She was in tight jean shorts and a bathing suit top and had on a pair of Nike running shoes. She had a tasteful script tattoo on her stomach that said, God...something or other. I couldn't make it out from there. She had long, straight dark hair and the body of a triathlete.

"That's Ramona," Vincent said without turning his head. "You'd best stay away from that."

Just then, Marty came out with a plate of hamburgers.

"Hey, Char," he bellowed.

He set down the hamburgers and came over and shook my shoulders.

"You're leg looks better," I said.

He had on shorts, flip-flops, and a Lions jersey that had double zeros on it, his huge shoulders straining the stitching. His face was more round than I remembered it and covered with salt and pepper stubble. The layup hadn't been kind to him.

"You two've met?" he asked.

Vincent Knight bent his neck as if he had a metal rod strapped to his spine and looked over at Marty. It was a seemingly normal situation on a seemingly normal day in an otherwise normal city, but the two men in front of me did not resemble humans so much as androids whose wires had begun to rust and whose brains were beginning to fry. They were trying to act normal, but they never would be.

What came to mind as I stood on the deck, beer in one hand, hamburger in the other, contemplating my situation, was a mountain climber who had said about mountains, "Once you start climbing you can't stop, and hitting the peak is no solace—90 percent of all accidents happen on the way down."

5

Marty explained to Vincent who I was and the favor I had done him. Gangs of all kinds, including the mafia, are suffering from competition, like any business where copious amounts of money are made. Finding and getting quality members and associates is not easy, especially in the criminal underworld. I was being recruited, which had been the whole point of Operation Sucker Punch.

Vincent waved off Marty as if he'd heard the story before, and then eyed me suspiciously, his bulbous eyes red and distant. He was high on something, but what I couldn't tell. Anyone with romantic notions of bikers need only meet one firsthand, smell the sour odor of a body decaying in alcohol abuse, see the dead, compassionless eyes, feel his clammy, icy handshake to know there is no romance there.

"What do you do?" Vincent asked, his raspy voice stringing his words together almost unintelligibly.

"About what?" I asked, unsmiling.

The humor went over Vincent's head. He stared at me blankly.

"He means, what do you do for a living?" Marty said.

"Whatever I can," I answered. "I've been back from Afghanistan for two years, finally have the injuries under control, but now I need to make some dough-re-me, and fast."

Vincent smiled, exposing a row of teeth so perfectly straight and white, it was clear they were dentures. A tinge of yellow would have made them look more real.

"Talk to him," Vincent told Marty. "See where it goes. Give him a test. You'll think of something."

Vincent grabbed a burger off the plate with his huge, gnarled hand and turned and went through the crowd, past Ramona and into the house.

I looked at Marty and said, "I need to be tested?"

"Hey, he's the boss man. Period."

"Who's Ramona? What's her story?"

"Vincent's niece."

"She single?" I asked.

Marty's eyes widened at that question. He looked over at her for a second and then looked into my eyes and said, "She's a hard nut to crack. No one's done it yet."

"She a carpet banger? How old is she?"

"Maybe. Twenty-seven."

"What's she do?" I asked.

"About what?" he shot back, grinning from ear to ear. "Nah, she has a foot fetish Internet site, has trolling vids on YouTube and a member site where people buy her clips, photos, and used socks and stockings. It's fucking retarded the money she makes."

"People make a living doing that?"

"That's her Hummer out front. Should see her penthouse condo off Lonsdale."

Ramona's eyes caught mine, and she picked up her margarita and came over to us.

"Who's the new blood, Marty?" she asked, looking at me the whole while.

"Ramona, Char. Char, Ramona."

Ramona extended her hand to shake mine. Her nails were French manicured, her grip stronger than Vincent's. Now I could see the script tattoo on her stomach: *God help you*.

That's funny. She didn't look religious.

"Do aerobics in your sleep?" I asked.

She laughed and said, "I go to an MMA gym in North Van."

"Was it Gauguin who said he liked a woman who could say I love you and then bust his teeth?"

She made a proper fist.

"You train?" she asked after noticing the Japanese symbols tattooed on my neck and visible above my jacket collar.

I said nothing.

"Oh, he's been known to bang," Marty said. "He's the guy that helped me out in the parking lot downtown."

Ramona looked me up and down, nearly licking her lips. I couldn't help but feel it was a show. She had a perfectly beautiful and exotic face but a hardness to her that belied her young life. I imagined she was a handful for any man. You'd have to have confidence coming out your ass even to approach her.

"Maybe you could come down to the gym, check it out," she said to me.

I could smell Ramona now. She smelled like strawberries and jasmine. I nodded and sipped my beer, like I didn't care. I did. I looked directly into her eyes, which were turquoise, like a high-elevation mountain lake.

I gave her my phone number, which she input into her iPhone.

"Call me when you're going," I told her.

She smiled and sipped her drink, then spun on the heels of her Nikes, and headed back to the chair where she had been sitting and chatting with an older, nondescript woman.

"Smooth move, Ex-lax," Marty said. "Didn't Vincent tell you to stay away?"

"I figured it was a suggestion, not an order."

Marty shook his head, said, "Tch-tch," and laughed a little, sounding like a little girl. It was the kind of giddy belly laugh that indicated he had never had many of those. It was a laugh rooted in the pain that underscored his reality.

"Look man," he whispered, taking me to the edge of the deck by tugging on my jacket sleeve. "I want to talk about something before I get too wasted. If you want, I have some work for you. Marc and I need some backup on a job next Thursday, someone behind us to snipe a few warning shots while we deal down."

I shrugged, doing my best to look nonchalant, and said, "Sure, give me the lowdown and I'll take care of it. What's the pay rate?"

"One G-note for two hours work, and lots more where that came from. You can do that kind of work, can't you? You were in the military."

"Not everyone in the military can snipe, but I can. Wait here," I said.

I set down my beer and ran to my car, popped the boot, and got my crossbow and a couple of arrows and took it out back and stood on the lawn below the deck. The crossbow got everyone's attention. Marty came down onto the lawn. Vincent came out of the house and leaned against the railing and lit a cigar with a silver lighter shaped like the Olympic torch. Ramona stood, a curious smile shaping her face. She came down the stairs and stood with Marty and me.

About fifty feet away was a shed with a cinderblock foundation. Using a piece of charcoal from the Kingsford bag, I scratched onto it a small bull's eye and then went back to the foot of the stairs.

I took Ramona's margarita from her and sipped from it, noting the lipstick marks she had left and making a show of putting my lips where hers had touched the glass. I patted the grass to make sure it was dry, sat, and positioned myself with the crossbow, loaded it and eyed the target. A few murmurs rippled through the small gathering. I fired the arrow.

Schtwack! The arrow went straight down the pipe and through the bull's eye, penetrating the cement block. The crowd cheered and went over to the shed. The end of the arrow stuck out maybe five inches. I got up and went over with them. Ramona reached down and flexed the shaft.

"That's the first time anyone's seen Ramona do that," someone said to the group. Laughter rose and fell. Ramona ignored the comment.

I went over to her, picked her up under her armpits, and set her down on the arrow, which supported her full weight, then stood back, and took out my camera. Ramona posed as much as she could, a huge smile on her face, and said, "wait," and took off her shoes and posed on the arrow first in her socks, and then in her bare feet. "Take close ups."

I took a dozen pictures for her with my digital camera.

"You have to e-mail me those photos," she said to me as I focused the lens on her arched feet straining to stay on the arrow shaft.

She got down from the arrow and put her socks and shoes back on. We shared another snort of her drink. When I turned around again, Vincent was staring at me, his hulking frame like a building blocking the warmth of the sun. He let out a cloud of cigar smoke and smiled. I'd never know what to make of his smiles. I think the Lone Wolves' boss man smiled at times because he anticipated others expected it. It's something sociopaths do to fool people into thinking they're normal, and to get what they want.

6

A few days later I checked out Ramona's Web site to get a bead on what I was dealing with. She had a page for every type of foot fetishist, and I learned real quick that, even within something as specific as that, there are those who want painted toes and those who want au natural, those who prefer runners and socks and those who prefer stockings and heels. There are also those who expect verbal abuse, humiliation, and financial fuckery. Ramona did not discriminate. She provided it all, to whoever was willing to pay. The videos and photos were shot in elegant surroundings, with light Italian marble and fine antique furniture and fancy cars on cobblestone drives, her feet on the pedals of course. The production value was high. Ramona was a dirty girl.

My experience with this type of sex trade worker was that sex was no longer about relationships or love, but about control, manipulation, and power. It was all too likely she had come from an abusive home. With Vincent Knight as her uncle, it was no surprise. At least with her site she could be on the controlling end of that stick.

Vincent Knight began to invade my mind and mornings in a wholly unexpected way, overlying the chimera that greeted me each morning, the one with the Afghan pedophile in it. Knight's image had replaced the Afghan's. It wasn't a stretch. In fact, there were great similarities between them, especially the bulging red eyes, the long hair, the beard and the cold, stoned demeanor. Both made money off heroin, too, probably.

When the image in my mind began to drift like stench in wind, I looked up from my bed out the window to the thin clouds scudding across a powder blue sky. I rolled to my side and could feel the semblance of pain, like needles in my lower back, spreading fear upward. I reached for the neurotransmitter control and cranked up the knob a few notches and felt my spine vibrate while the needles dissipated. The daymares I could take, as long as this fucking piece of electronic shit kept at bay the nightmare of debilitating pain.

My BlackBerry Torch phone was on the dresser, and when it rang, it got me up out of bed. It was Marty.

"Today's the day," he said, his voice croaky, like he'd drunk too much or stayed out too long.

"What's the plan?" I asked. I got up and walked to the can and lifted the lid and pissed while I spoke to him.

"Meet me and Marc in Steveston, at the Tim Horton's on Steveston Highway. Bring whatever you need."

"What time?"

"Nine tonight."

As soon as I ended the call, I went to the kitchen to start the coffee. My phone rang again.

"Hello?"

"Is this crossbow man?" a sexy voice asked, a voice that sounded like silk caressing inner thigh.

"Hey, girl, sleep off the margaritas yet?"

"Long ago, my friend, long ago. Listen," she said, all business, "I'm headed to the gym to do a little cardio and sparring. Care to join me, meet some of my boys?"

"Can you take a punch?" I joked.

She was silent for a moment, then laughed quietly, condescendingly, then gave me directions to the gym, which was on Lonsdale, north of Victoria Park, and said, "I'll meet you in the parking lot at the side, so you don't have to go in alone."

I doubted the gym was hard-core, like the ones I'd visited in Vegas or L.A., but it was a good idea to go in with her. There are a lot of egos strutting in the gyms nowadays, and a lot of gangbangers. I was bound to be outnumbered.

I made a shake with protein powder and mixed berries, drank that down, packed my gym bag, and headed out. I had a long way to go from New Westminster and arrived ten minutes late, just after two in the afternoon. Ramona was leaning against the fender of her yellow Hummer when I pulled into the stall beside her. She was wearing a tight black warm-up suit that looked fantastic on her hard-muscled body. Her hair was in a pony tail, and she had a small gym bag slung over her shoulder. She didn't recognize me as the driver till I got out and looked at her over the roof of the Skyline.

"Jeezuz, nice ride," she said, her eyes making love to the lines. "What the fuck is it?"

"It's the fastest motherfucking car in the lower mainland—that's what it is."

She ran the palm of her hand over the fender and bent to look inside.

"You'll have to give me a ride, if you can move after the workout."

"Sure. You can come for a spin in the car, too," I said, wisecracking.

She ignored that comment, squinted at me as if to challenge me, and then blew a playful kiss, which I caught and slapped on my ass as we stepped into the gym.

There wasn't even a sign advertising the existence of the low-budget affair that had once been a dance studio. Tinted windows along the front didn't allow you to see in. This place was strictly word of mouth.

Ramona directed me to the men's change room while two men in headgear nodded to her and watched me standing beside her. There were only a dozen lockers, two showers, and a toilet and urinal, but it was relatively clean, well stocked, without dirty towels lying around and no pooled water or urine on the tiled floor. I put on a pair of white and bright pink fight shorts, set the mouth guard behind my left ear, and went out to the gym and got straight on the stationary bike, hoping someone would say something ignorant about the shorts.

Ramona was not in the gym yet. I could hear her voice from the women's locker room, sounding as though she was talking on the phone. There were four men at the cage, two wearing head gear and sparring inside it, two yelling instructions from the other side of the chain link fence.

After fifteen minutes on the bike, I did a quick aerobic circuit on the Universal and worked the dumbbells, then stood in front of the mirror and sparred, floating on the balls of my feet. Finally Ramona came out wearing a black sports bra, black and white fight pants, and carrying a skipping rope.

"Sorry. I got a call I had to deal with." She noticed the burn scars marbled across the breadth of my torso. "Holy shit, man. What happened to you?"

The scars weren't glaringly contrasted, but once you saw them, you couldn't help but wonder.

"I'm here to work out, not socialize," I said, ignoring her.

Ramona went to the far side of the mats and began to skip. The sparring in the cage stopped. The two men outside the cage were eyeing my shadow boxing. One of them came over to Ramona and spoke to her while she jumped rope.

"Hey, Char, this is Bill. Bill McVee," Ramona said through her breath. "He owns the gym. Bill, that's new blood, Char. Guess where he gets his name?"

Bill came over, his eyes on the fight shorts rather than the skin. He was about 5'9", 190 pounds. He had the thick chest of a freestyle wrestler and had a large, protruding forehead and attentive, intelligent eyes. His hair, like most MMA fighters, was shaved to the wood. He had an unoriginal barbed-wire tattoo band around his right bicep and a symbol like a family crest on his breastplate.

Bill extended his hand to shake mine. He looked now at the burn marks across my chest and at the Japanese symbols on my neck, but said nothing.

"Care to spar? We could use a fresh look."

"Depends."

"On?"

In a large gym, you could never walk in and challenge hierarchy without dire consequences. This was not a large gym, though. From the look of the pugs in the cage, I suspected gangbangers. It was probably a toy they laundered money through. Still, I didn't want trouble, yet.

"The level of your game. I don't want to step on any toes. Just stand up or anything goes?"

Ramona had stopped skipping and was looking over at us with interest. Had this been her plan all along? Maybe it had been a test assigned by Vincent.

"He trains Manny Rio," she said of Bill McVee.

Rio was in my file, but I had no idea what that meant. It didn't matter.

"What's your training?" Bill asked me.

"Kyukoshin. Knock down karate. Catch wrestling. Throws and blows."

McVee's eyes clouded with confusion.

"Catch wrestling," I said. "As in 'catch as catch can.' Started in England in the 1800s, with miners fighting for bets. It spread to Europe and eventually Japan. It's the basis for Shooto, the MMA tournament that preceded UFC."

He still looked confounded.

"What's your training?" I asked him.

"All–Canadian freestyle wrestler, boxing, BJJ."

BJJ came almost without mentioning. If you fought MMA, you needed BJJ or some other form of submission fighting, like catch wrestling. The other arts were interchangeable.

McVee looked me up and down again and said, "Suit up. I'll meet you in center cage in five."

I was about to get my shine on. I shrugged and bit down on my mouthpiece. Ramona was holding the rope at her side and looking at me doubtfully. What she liked about this situation was that she thought she was in control, manipulating me, manipulating Bill, perhaps seeing where I stood or initiating me into her world.

Someone was about to learn a lesson.

7

I taped my own hands and slipped on the training gloves and had Ramona lace them for me. She stood back to look at me, then bent, and ran her fingers over an old blood stain on the shorts.

"Not mine," I said.

I usually trained only with Pop and his select students, so the quiet gym did not distract me. I entered the octagon and went to the far side and regarded McVee with his training partners, both small but ripped Filipinos, who looked over at me excitedly, impatient for my supposed beat down.

McVee entered the cage looking stoic. His friends closed and locked the gate behind him. He came to my side of the cage, touched gloves with me, and lisped through his mouthpiece, "Full speed on everything but locks."

I nodded. That was fine with me. I hadn't planned on using any. I wouldn't need them.

The bell rang at cage side, and McVee sprinted across the cage toward me.

I sidestepped to my right and moved quickly around the outside of the ring and let him stalk me, keeping my distance about twice that of the average fighter—two meters maybe. He kept his hands high, tight, his chin tucked, his torso leaning forward. He had good technique, but not excellent. We'd see if that would deteriorate along with his cardio.

McVee swung a jab-straight-hook combo that was a foot and a half away. I leapt with a double high-low kick. Both landed squarely. I moved away again, angled to his right, and then switched to southpaw.

"Cut him off into the corner!" McVee's partner yelled. "Lead with a kick!"

He did that and attempted a shot, but he was too far away. With my forearms on his shoulders, I planted him on the mat, and then stood back, ready to change tactics. When I was certain his hand speed was not a threat, I moved into the pocket and landed a few combos of my own, took a glancing hook on the chin, then moved to my left, and hit him with a front kick to the liver when he tried to shoot.

"Get him against the cage!" Ramona yelled.

I wasn't sure who she was yelling at. McVee probably.

Within two minutes, I had hit McVee with a dozen combos, pulling the punches, and an equal number of high and low kicks, had stuffed two takedown attempts, and had hip-tossed him, which caused his eyes to open wide. His third takedown try was from six feet away. He just didn't have the speed to close on me. I used my forearms again to separate us, and he was in the perfect position for a Thai clinch. I knew a wrestler would welcome a clinch.

I locked my fingers behind his neck and knew what the wrestler was thinking: "Ah, the clinch. Now we're in my world." We weren't.

It can take years to learn the clinch and how to get out of it, how to become proficient at defending a technique that to outsiders looks simple to avoid or defend. McVee didn't have the footwork. The look on his face went from stoic confidence to puzzlement to terror when I began to turn and knee his midsection. His mind was on preventing the body blows, so I wrenched him sideways, got him off balance, and took him to the cage and rag-dolled him as I kneed his liver. After a dozen shots, he brought his arms down to protect himself. I aimed through his face to the back of his head, and the knee dropped him straight to the mat.

I'd been careful not to hit his nose. That could have killed him. His friends rushed into the cage to help McVee onto his back. I leaned in and put my hand on his stomach, which was heaving with breath. I noticed that his mouthpiece had flown out and had lodged into the chain links. I stood up tall, hands on hips, and looked through the fence at Ramona. She was standing with her hands on the cage, the skipping rope dangling down, a smile etched ever so slightly across her lips.

Maybe I wasn't the one she'd intended to punk. Maybe it was McVee all along.

McVee sat up, and within a couple of minutes, he seemed fine. He had no idea what had happened, didn't even recognize me. That's what a good KO'll do: erase the last ten minutes of your life.

I stepped from the cage once McVee was standing and warmed down next to Ramona while she finished her circuit, wondering what, if anything, the boys would do about the beating. I wasn't a ringer: I'd told McVee my credentials, and he'd seen me working out, which was precisely why he wanted a shot at me. I sensed all of it was a test, perhaps one sent down from the man himself, Vincent Knight.

"We can shower back at my place," Ramona said while wiping sweat from her brow with a small towel.

Ramona's penthouse condo was in a luxury six-story cement, steel, and glass structure a half block west of Lonsdale in expensive North Van. Her wrap around, bi-level balcony looked down the hill to the inlet and west toward Georgia Strait. The light Italian marble and the exquisite antique furnishings were familiar to me from her Web site.

The shower stall in Ramona's en suite was spacious enough to turn a horse, and the walk from there to the toilet was a bit of a stroll. I showered first, and then she. I was in her bedroom admiring her Danish bedroom furniture and watching a cargo ship drift in the distance when Ramona came out of the bathroom and onto the bedroom carpet. When I turned, I was surprised to see her naked, her hair wet and dishevelled, her arms wrapping me.

She kissed me flush. I kissed her back, not as passionately at first, but I gave it a try. She let go her grip on me and leaned back to apprise me.

"What's this?" she said, fingering the remote for the neurotransmitter that was clipped to my belt.

"Insta-sanity," I said. I explained it to her.

She listened with a kind of disconnection, took my arm, and dragged me to the bed. I was fully clothed, and she was naked, and it wasn't all bad, but Ramona could sense discomfort in my rigidity.

Ramona began to unbutton my shirt and pants and pulled them off for me and then lay me down on the bed and took from her bedside table strips of soft cloth and ran them through rings on the four corners of the bed. I lay on my back, unwilling to stop whatever Ramona had in store for me. I complied for the same reason I had said yes to Vulture: after Afghanistan, the edges of sanity were the only boundaries where existence for me was worthwhile.

8

When Ramona was finished with me an hour later, after instructing me on the finer points of oral service, she left me tied to her bed while she went to the kitchen. When she returned, she had a glass of cranberry juice, and she drank that while looking me over like I was a domestic chore she rued. She could have done anything she'd wanted to me, which was precisely what I enjoyed about it. She had a look of boredom on her face, though. I presumed few lived up to her expectations.

I guessed it was around six. The thought occurred to me that I would need to get ready for my rendezvous with Marty.

"Do you want up?" she asked, the glass empty in her hands.

I had to bend my neck to look at her, which I did momentarily, but with my head back down on the bed, I said what she needed to hear: "Not particularly. You'll let me up when you're good and ready."

The image of her taut, tattooed stomach and muscular thighs wrapped around my face would die with me. I dreaded what I might do to get it. She sensed my furthered excitement and laughed a surprisingly soft and muted laugh.

"Don't worry," she said. "You'll get to your meeting. But you have more work to do. You're not going to see my face for another hour."

By the time I left Ramona's, she was in her office uploading videos to her site and uninterested in my presence. I let myself out and raced home to get the bullpup M89-SR sniper rifle I kept in my gun safe in my bedroom closet. I opened up the carbon-fiber case. Along with the rifle were a detachable night scope, bipod, and quick-detachable silencer for those low-noise jobs. On the top shelf, I found a dozen subsonic rounds and gathered those up. I checked the parts of the rifle, took it apart again, locked it all up, and headed out and placed the gun in a hidden compartment below the trunk floor, which would fool a cursory look if I was pulled over, but not a thorough inspection. It was eight fifteen. I called Marty on his cell and told him I was on my way.

Traffic in my direction was moderate, and I pulled into the lot off Steveston Highway and reached the Tim Horton's with five minutes to spare. I backed into a stall and saw Marty and another man inside the restaurant sitting at a table near a window.

Odd place to meet, I thought.

I got out and headed inside. The air was warm enough considering the sky was clear and summer had not yet come. Marty saw me walking up and waved at me like he was a friend.

I went inside and went over to their table. Marty had on black jeans and a Storm Surf hoodie.

"Char, Marc. Marc, Char," Marty said, introducing us.

I shook Marc's hand as I sat. Each had a coffee. I didn't, but I just wanted to get down to the case.

Marc Glasner was not a tall man but a very muscular man. He looked like he'd be no taller than 5'6", but his arms strained the denim jacket he wore. I knew from the file he was a full-patch member of the Lone Wolves and that he was a loner, fended for himself. In 2009, the VPD had to have a sit-down with Vincent to reign in the fuck, who had been wielding his patch with too much abandon, terrorizing the downtown Eastside. His gnarled knuckles and cauliflower ears were a warning sign to any intelligent comers that you didn't fuck lightly with Marc. He smelled like motorcycle oil.

"I heard you helped the man, here," Marc said to me, a surprisingly sophisticated French accent rolling off his tongue.

He must be from France, I thought, not Quebec, where they all sounded as if they'd just got off the boat three hundred years ago.

"I'm not into unfair fights," I said, acting bored.

I looked around me. The bright fluorescents in the coffee shop depressed me.

"Can we get out of here?" I asked. Pop lived nearby, and it would be my luck to run into him or someone I knew from the neighborhood. "I feel like a spotlight's shining on me."

Marc and Marty stood and took up their to-go cups. I went with them out the door to Marty's pewter Tundra. He opened the driver's door and reached inside and took out a printout of a Google map.

"The deal's on Dyke Road. *X* marks the spot. *Y* marks you." He smiled, like that was funny. "It's slightly elevated with a clear view, near a copse of trees. No one around."

"What the fuck's a copse?" Marc asked Marty.

Marty ignored him and with a smirk on his lips said to me, "You're there in case we get a little attitude. We've been getting attitude lately. We're just getting cash owed us. Should be in a duffle. If there's any grief, I'll slick back my hair with my right hand. That's your sign to pick something off, like a side mirror."

"On their car or yours?"

Ignoring that comment, Marty said, "If I use my left, pick someone off. I don't care who. They should have two men, but lately they've been breaking protocol. You're scoped, right."

"Of course," I answered.

"Just asking," he said. "Just making sure."

I looked at Marc as he stood with his back to me, watching a BMW pull into the lot, driven by a kid who looked twelve. Marc's hair was thin and wet looking, accentuating a bald spot for all but him to see. He was really short, as wide as he was tall, didn't seem to suffer from small-man syndrome, but he had to. Something about him was off, way off. Anyone would have keyed on it. There were no laugh lines on his face, and something in his brain was unplugged. He turned and caught me watching him, as if he had sensed me staring at him.

"How'd you two meet?" I asked him, hoping to diffuse the awkwardness.

Marc looked blankly at me.

Marty said, "'Bout fifteen years ago. We were both strikers. We patched on the same day."

The gang is often the only semblance of family guys like this have ever had. Marc excused himself and went to the washroom in the Tim Horton's. I noticed a slight limp and asked Marty about it.

"Three years in to the stint, Marc stole a custom Harley from downtown thinking it'd impress the brass. Vincent knew the owner and returned the bike, then had Marc beaten with a choker chain," he said, sipping his coffee as if that was the most normal thing in the world. Maybe in his world it was. He pulled up his hood.

"Take off, my man," Marty said, looking at his watch. "The meeting's set up for ten. Do not fuck up."

"You just better hope one of them doesn't show up in a black Storm Surf hoodie," I said.

When he laughed, he snorted. As I turned to go to my car, my eye caught the gleam of his nickel-plated .44 shoved into his belt, its icy reflection no match for the coldness in his eye.

9

The clump of fir and old arbutus Marty had indicated on the map was 150 meters from where Marty stopped his Tundra. When the truck lights went off, I had already parked and had the rifle resting on the bipod. The night scope worked brilliantly. From that distance, I could count Marc's nose hairs—and he was French so there were plenty. I could see their breath in the cool, moist air next to the Fraser, which flowed on the other side of the dyke.

If the ice sheets ever do melt, I thought, this whole fucking delta is unsalvageable ocean floor.

There was a little breeze in the air, coming from the southeast, just enough that I might have to use a little wind-age. It didn't matter. With this weapon and from this distance, I could plug a neat hole through an eye-glass lens.

Peering through the scope, I could see exaggerated tension on Marc's face, on the wrinkled lines on his forehead. The two Lone Wolves spoke angrily for a couple of seconds before Marty turned and looked directly at me, even though I knew he couldn't see me.

A Subaru Impreza rolled down Dyke Road right on time. I could hear the base thumping through the night air from where I lay. I breathed evenly and deeply. My heart rate increased when four Asian men stepped from the car, a metallic briefcase in the lead's hands. None of the men were large, intimidating, or tough looking, but that was part of their success.

I recognized the man in the lead. He was Lyle Ng, head of the Red-Legged Tarantulas, a gang of mostly Vietnamese and Chinese immigrants, a gang that only five years ago had been a gnat on the Lone Wolves' faces but was now considerable in number. I knew the gang as primary distributers for the Lone Wolves, and rivals of the MPs, a gang of mixed races but primarily Filipinos and East Indians.

Ng held the briefcase and stood at an angle to Marc, without looking the least bit interested in handing it over. Bringing four men was not something Marty had agreed to, but he kept his cool, didn't raise his hand to slick back his hair. I kept my eye on an Asian who stood furthest back, who seemed to be nervous about something.

The Lone Wolves were typically above the kinds of violence that had been reaching the newsstands lately. They had more sophisticated ways of lethal coercion—contractors like me—and let the minions below them duke it out. But where there are drugs and copious amounts of cash, someone will try horning in, or at least someone will eventually try ripping you off. No one had yet been implicated in the recent gangland murders plaguing Vancouver, which everyone knew was a gang war for turf, especially in the face of the wars down in Mexico and the depleted flow of drugs and cash that had resulted. The system was bottlenecked, and those at street level were fighting over what was getting through. New sources were sought. That's why I had been hired: to find that new source.

Marty never raised his hand, but the thin, wiry Asian in the shadows pulled from his jacket what looked to me like a micro-submachine gun. I gently squeezed the trigger and in utter silence saw through the scope the gun fly out of Jackie Chan's hand and skid under the Subaru. In that instant, Marty and Marc drew their .44s.

Marty took the briefcase from Ng, opened it, and looked inside it while the Asian men backed off, peering into the darkness, but there had not been the least noise to point my direction.

I could smell the burnt heat from the round mingling with the peaty aroma emanating from the ground, ran my palm lovingly over the stalk of the rifle. I kept an eye on the scene, though, and while three of the Asian men piled back into the Subaru, Marc held Ng with one arm and wagged a finger in his face, his steamy breath enveloping the smaller man.

Lights flitted behind them. A car was approaching in the distance, still a ways off. Marc and Marty got back in the Tundra. Ng went to the driver's side of the Subaru, stepped into it, and in an instant, he had fired up the engine, revved it, and spun the tires and the car, drifting it perfectly around and then smoking all four tires as it shot down the road, passing the oncoming vehicle before it had turned a corner and reached Marty. The Tundra sat quiet and motionless. That's when I noticed the car was an RCMP cruiser.

I disassembled the rifle, placed all the parts in its case, set the whole thing in the trunk compartment, closed the lid, and got in the car and backed it up, knowing full well the cops in the cruiser would be able to see my lights from there.

The cop car stopped opposite the Tundra, but I couldn't worry about that now. I'd done my job. I thought it might be fun to boot down the road and head up to Steveston Highway. Maybe I could find the Subaru. I'd be able to spot it a mile away.

I wasn't able to find the Tarantulas, but I circled back to the spot where they'd met with Marty and Marc, got out of my car, and felt the eerie stillness in the air, the latent, quiet power of the river. I used my keychain light to illuminate the grass near the edge of the road. After a minute or two, I found the gun, a 9mm TEC9—an honest mistake from that distance, in the dark. The round had hit the trigger guard so the weapon would still be functional.

I picked it up, placed it in the trunk compartment, and got back in and headed for home, dreading not the night but the morning daymares that arose with every sun.

10

When I got home I poured myself a shot of Jack Damage, slid that down my gullet, poured another, and sipped on that with the TV on. I stared numbly at UFC Unleashed while thinking about Ramona. I was happy to have her for now: I wasn't willing to have a normal relationship, so I might as well have fun while it lasted, if it lasted.

Despite the fact that the neurotransmitter was working well and had been for some time, my greatest fear was that, like all the other treatments and drugs I'd used, eventually my body would become immune to its effects. It was a road I couldn't stand to go down again. At this point, the efforts I'd made, the treatments I'd tried, were a hodgepodge, reactions to the phenomenon that was always in control. The most frustrating aspect was that none of the specialists seemed to know what was happening to me. Like many veterans, I often felt like I was standing alone. Welcome to difficult-to-diagnose chronic pain.

I'd never been much of a planner anyhow. That's why I had fit in so much better into life at war in Afghanistan than I ever had at home here in Canada. Brazen opportunists and arseholes excel in war; meticulous planners succeed in peace. As I drank down the last of the second shot and poured a third, I hoped Vulture was right and that this line of "work" would satisfy that hugely dysfunctional aspect to my psyche.

Around midnight, my cell rang. I hoped it was Ramona, but it was Marty.

"Good job," he said. "Didn't see the fucker behind Ng with the meat grinder."

"Don't send thanks, send money," I said, sipping more of the whiskey, my own voice sounding slurred.

"No problem. Come by the digs, and I'll have your cash, maybe a little bonus."

"I picked up their TEC9. Know anyone who wants it?"

"Yeah, man. Whadday want for it?"

"Eight large."

"Bring it with you when you come."

I had a terrible night attempting sleep. The JD hadn't helped a lick. Even though the transmitter wiped out the searing pain that often enveloped my body like electrified red-hot barbed wire, what remained was a residual and overall nausea and ill will, a haunting ghost of the real thing that seemed to have as its core every cell in my body, robbing me of joy or rest. It didn't happen every day, but rose and fell like ocean groundswell, just as unpredictably.

Around three a.m. I sat on the edge of my mattress in a rhombus of moonlight that spotlighted the edge of the bed, my sheets knotted into a fist, suppressing a scream that I desperately needed to let out. I planted my face into the pillow and with gritted teeth yelled, "FUCK!" as loud as I could, as many times as I could till the belief that it would help subsided.

I put on my satin robe—at these times, I avoided anything too scratchy on my skin—and shuffled to the kitchen and made myself a grilled cheese sandwich. Filling my stomach was usually the best medicine for falling asleep again. I followed that with a large glass of lemon water, and when I went back to bed, I fell right asleep.

When the phone rang at ten the next morning, it woke me. This time it was Ramona.

"You're not stalking me, are you?" I joked.

"Yeah, like I need to stalk anyone. Say, what are you doing Friday?"

"What do you want me to be doing?" I said, playing her like a viola.

"Always the right thing to say," Ramona said, friendly enough but an untrustworthy lilt to her voice.

"How's McVee's ego?" I asked.

"He'd be angrier if he remembered what happened."

I chuckled at that comment.

"Who were you trying to punk, me or him?"

"Hey, I just thought you might like to work out with me. You seemed like my kind of guy."

I didn't believe her.

"Seemed?" I asked.

"Seem," she said.

"I don't know. Your type likes to scheme. Something was going on there. Someone was being tested. Maybe even you."

My foray into her mind yielded dividends, but my last comment diffused her.

"I'm having a few people over this weekend. Thought you'd like to come over, help me set up."

This was the first morning in a long while when I hadn't woken up forced to relive my Afghan nightmare, all because of a conversation with a dangerously sexy woman.

"I give," I said. "But what kind of party we talking about? Gangbangers and muscle heads who think they're a lot tougher than they are?"

"No one in your league, babe," was her response.

I hung up the phone happily enough, but I knew nothing ever went well when you tied yourself to a woman like Ramona. The depth of her mind was dark and hidden, like the great mass of ice that comprised the burgs that cruised past Newfoundland after berthing in the Arctic Ocean. Hit one at your peril.

11

I glanced out the bathroom window as I went to bathe. It looked sunny and pleasant out, for anyone who'd give a shit. I knew my day was done. The day after a bad night was always ten times worse than my worst ever tequila hangover. Although I did shower, my skin couldn't take it on bad days. Baths were always less intrusive.

I came out of the tub feeling sleepy but a little better. I had some eggs over incorrigible with some sourdough toast and bacon with sliced tomatoes, washed it all down with an Incan coffee so thick and strong it was like you had dipped your cup into a Peruvian mud slide, and then went online to check the weather and to Google Ng.

The first link sent me to a page where Ng's short but prolific MMA career boasted a record of 14-1, against nothing but Western Canadian competition though. He'd fought no one from the States or anywhere else. He was an up and comer, had beaten a few Albertans who'd made it to King of the Cage and a few other decent organizations. His style was JKD, which meant almost anything. JKD fighters, the ones who actually followed Lee's sage advice rather than blowing hot air, used what worked for them, in whatever mix and make-up benefited their size, weight, build, and athletic ability. That was Lee's screed, and mine too. I searched YouTube and found some grainy vids of Ng fighting in Edmonton, Calgary, and Red Deer. His frame reminded me of Viet Cong fighters: lean, wiry muscles like rope. He was a tough fighter, much stronger than he appeared physically, with abundant energy. He wasn't a big man and didn't have much weight behind him. His tactic was punches in bunches. He seemed pretty good at hitting buttons. He had ten KOs, his only loss a split decision. When he fought anyone with good wrestling, he protected himself well while on his back, in the guard, but that wouldn't work well against me in a back lot.

I put my laptop to sleep and got dressed. Just as I was about to leave, the phone rang again. It was Pop.

"Char? That doesn't sound like you."

Pop called me Char not just because he, too, caught on to the nickname, but because my actual name was Charles. It was an easy adjustment for everyone.

"I had a bad night last night," I told him. "I'm better now."

"You keep up the meditation I showed you?" he said. "Can't hurt."

"I can't ever sit still," I told him. "It wasn't just the shell that got fried."

Pop had been more devastated than I when I got wheeled off the transport in Trenton. He changed the subject.

"When are you coming out to train? We need your body."

Pop had the slight and forceful Japanese accent and high cheekbones that made you think military, although he hadn't been happy when I'd enlisted. He'd tried to talk me out of it. He was a proud man who felt comfortable in the small Japanese community in Steveston that had begun with the formation of the fish plants there along the Fraser.

"Sunday," I said. "I'll come out Sunday."

Pop cleared his throat and said, "Are you doing okay? Do you need any money?"

I still received a low monthly stipend from the Canadian Armed Forces, but I hadn't told him about my new employment. I hadn't known how to broach it because if he hadn't liked my joining the army, he certainly wouldn't like this job and the people it put me in contact with. Also, I didn't want to involve him in any way. I even wondered if I should cut off contact with him altogether until the job was done, but that wasn't possible. He was all I had for grounding. But I'd have to explain the newfound cash flow.

"I'm fine. I have some consulting work with the government," I said, clearing my throat and feeling proud of the misleading half-truth.

Silence.

"I spoke to mom last week," I told him, to steer the conversation away from my work.

Mom was the elephant in our room. She had left him for a Seattle businessman when I was three, left me with him. Neither of us cared for her. She was and always had been all about herself, her gratification, and her two packs a day and her "two" vodkas with dinner.

"Is she well?" he asked, unconcerned.

"Still alive, apparently separated from Philip."

"HA!" Pop blurted, but he avoided saying anything further about it. "So, Sunday then. What time?"

"One," I said. "See you then, Pop."

"Bye, son."

I put the phone down and stood by the living room window with the dregs of coffee and stared out over the Fraser, which was grey and turbid under the high, blue sky. In the surge an eddy emerged and, bobbing within it, the undercarriage of an automobile, itself grey and no match for the colossal power of the mighty river.

I left at noon to head to Marty's, to pick up the cash for the job and the TEC9—a cool 1,800 clams, but first I had a few errands to run in town. I hadn't gotten two blocks from home when a black-and-white pulled me over, the officer claiming I looked suspicious.

"What, was I going the speed limit, signalling to turn?"

I sweated bullets. It never ceases to amaze me how fate can befall like an anvil dropping from the sky. The policeman was alone, no taller than 6'9" and no wider than a meat wagon. His face was round and puffy from steroid abuse, his eyes soft and damp. He searched the interior, putting his hands under my seats, and had me pop the boot. He found the compartment in the trunk where I'd kept the guns.

"What's this?" he asked, picking up the satchel.

"A laptop," I said, looking him straight in his dairy-cow eyes. "I keep it there, out of view. I've had one laptop stolen already. Never again."

He opened the zip, closed it, and returned the bag and closed the compartment and trunk lid. A look of frustration came over his face.

How did he find the compartment so easily? I wondered. It had been designed to be inconspicuous.

He stalled, unsure whether or not to let me go, but acquiesced at last.

When I drove away, I accelerated fast but not above the limit. In the rearview, I could see him standing on long, thick legs, his tree-trunk torso leaning to one side, his face contorted with ambiguity.

12

Marty's face looked worn and sullen, the skin dragging down the sides of his face, making him look like the Cowardly Lion. It was a tremendously surprising transformation. I suspect men like that regularly fall into emotional chasms, depressions they can't see coming. He was friendly enough to me though.

He wore a red, white, and silver Ohio State football jersey with the number ten on it and a pair of red Metal Mulisha fight shorts. He'd already had a bottle of Wild Turkey on the go when I got there. When he came out of the bedroom with a stack of wrinkled and bound bills, he handed it to me, and I put it in the Mickey pocket of my Caballero without counting it, which impressed him.

"Care for a shot?" he asked.

"I think I'd better."

"I think so too. You look like hell—like I should talk."

He poured me three fingers in a lowball, essentially filling it. I took a good gulp. It tasted thin and sweet. He sipped his almost grudgingly, rubbing the stubble on his chin and looking out the window at the field, past a row of trees to a silo in the distance.

Inside his home was a dump, with bottles from his last party still on the kitchen table and counter, and cigarette butts piled high in ashtrays and in things that passed for ashtrays. Somehow the room smelled like beer and ashes. A pair of worn sheer stockings lay on the carpet right in front of the 42" flat screen, which was showing the Barrett-Jackson auctions, sound off. A Daytona yellow '68 Corvette was up to seventy grand.

"I've got more work for you if you want," he said, his voice croaking. He sat down on a sectional that was way too soft for me to sit on. I stood, half facing him, half facing the window.

"I liked the last job. Give me a rifle, 150 meters, and a stack of bills, and I'm a happy camper."

Marty gulped from his Wild Turkey, his hand clenching the glass so tightly his knuckles turned white, no hint of a smile.

"Vincent senses your value," he said. "So do I. He needs you out there, walking the grey line. It doesn't hurt you look like you'd fit in with the Tarantulas or the MPs. He pays well, as you can see."

"You gotta know I have no interest in joining your... club, even if you wanted me. I'm a jobber here—that's it. When I get enough money, I might be gone."

"Hey, nothing wrong with money as a motivator, and more than half our clan are associates. With that comes special privileges, and special requirements."

I decided to ignore that.

"So what's the job?"

"You're going to Ramona's party Friday?"

"You know I am."

"Ng will be there. Think you can punk him?"

"Don't know," I said, thinking quietly. "If he's alone, yeah, but if he's with the posse, probably not. What's he doing there? This some big fraternity or something."

Marty looked up at me with his sagging jowls. "Or something," he said.

"I'll see what I can do," I told him at last.

That brightened him up a bit, enough to bring the glass to his face with a little hope in his eyes, but still no smile, as if the bourbon could douse whatever was burning inside his gut. He drank it down and set his glass on the only empty spot on the coffee table in front of him and refilled it. I could almost hear his fuse burning.

"Work him over a little, compliments of Vincent. Remind him who and what he is. He won't see you coming. Need to keep 'em off balance."

Within minutes, Marty began to meld into the sofa, his face becoming even more jowly. I could almost see his beard grow. I let myself out and walked to the Skyline with the hint of a buzz washing pleasantly over my body. Now that I was off most of the pharmaceuticals, I could enjoy my liquor here and there.

I stopped at a strip mall and picked up some sushi and ate that while I drove and thought about the strange smallness of the underworld, how everyone knew everyone and how they intermingled and intermarried like French queens had copulated with English kings, the difference being—well, there wasn't much difference. Criminals all.

When I got back to New West, I didn't feel like going straight home. I went to one of the antique shops on the corner and looked through their display cases, hoping something would pop. After forty minutes, I saw in the clutter on the second glass shelf a 1940s chromium corkscrew, with a broad, finger-grooved handle and stout screw. I let it float in the palm of my hand till it found the sweet spot, and then clenched my fist around it. Ideal. The jagged metal tip protruded three quarters of an inch. I paid the clerk twelve dollars, pocketed the corkscrew, and left the store.

When I got home, I counted the money—$1,800 on the nose. I had another drink, a Black Grouse, and headed back down to an antique jewellery store on Columbia Street, where I bought a white gold Bulova I'd had my eyes on and then headed across the street to The Heritage Grill, where I had a bite to eat. I was feeling pretty good, actually, which was a change. The work seemed easy, I finally had some cash flow happening, and I had a good meal on the plate in front of me. Nothing good lasts.

13

I arrived at Ramona's swanky North Van condo around eight, before any guests were expected. If I thought it would be a gathering of lowbrow imbeciles, I was at least partly wrong. Crystal punch bowls were strategically placed throughout her home, and a caterer was delivering seafood platters and snack trays. Ramona lived in an upscale building, after all, and wouldn't be able to hold a head-banger, which is what I had been expecting.

I could hear Ramona's voice coming from the kitchen, so I made my way over. She was wearing a beautiful turquoise and yellow dress and had on a pair of stockings, the seam as straight as a plumb line up the backs of her legs, and the highest stilettos I'd ever seen anyone prance in, matching blue with metallic spiked heels. She was facing an impossibly petite and attractive young, short-haired blonde with wide, innocent-looking eyes.

"Twelve hundred was generous, Mia," Ramona said, waving a wad of cash in front of the blonde. She ripped some bills off the top, shoved the rest into the Mia's hands and said, "Here's eight, then. Consider yourself lucky you get to lay on your back for me."

With that said, Ramona moved Mia aside with her arm and walked toward the living room, her stilettos clacking across the tiled floor, almost sparking, where a man was bent behind a stereo system trying to connect it to a Mac.

"I'm sorry," Mia said, her accent an odd mix, like a German speaking Bulgarian maybe. "I didn't mean to..."

Ramona stopped suddenly, spun with the effortless grace of a dancer on the balls of her feet, and stared a hole through the blonde, who visibly winced.

"You will be sorry. Get changed. Now!"

Mia scurried off. It was as if I was watching a play on a stage, and I almost laughed, but there was an authentic look of dread in Mia's eyes and one of cold meanness in Ramona's, which, at that moment, caught mine. If she was embarrassed about me being there, she didn't show it.

"Char, c'mon in," she said, her facial-muscle tension gone. "Want anything to drink? There's beer in the fridge and cooler, and there's a bar here."

She pointed to a long table that had been set up for drinks and food platters. Her large breasts and curvy hips drew the eyes down no matter how hard you tried to be civil.

"I'm up here, Char," she said, smiling slightly and pointing to her eyes.

The difference between a woman who thinks she can be dirty and a slut is that the former will blow you on Valentines Day, taking one for the team, whereas the latter can't stand another minute without someone's balls slapping her chin. Ramona was in between, but her dirtiness came in the form of her need to be acted upon, as if she couldn't stand another second without someone's face between her legs. Sex to her was control over another human. Put differently, control over other humans had replaced sex for her.

With party preparations under control, we spent an hour in her bedroom with the door locked. By the end of it, my tongue felt as if it had been ripped out and ridden over by a cement truck, and there were several red indentations over my torso and buttocks where Ramona had dug in her stiletto heel. She'd even dug her heels into the burn scars, a rapturous glow overtaking her whole body, a glow that enveloped her being whenever she imposed her will and whim on someone.

Being in bed with Ramona was a lot like riding the Kentucky Rumbler: you just didn't have time to think and, afterward, weren't sure if you'd screamed or not and just felt lucky to be alive. After she grinded herself into my face and stood above me smoothening her dress over her abdomen, she brought Mia in and had her blow me, and my mind. This was the addictive quality Ramona had, turning me into her little crack addict. Like a drug dealer, she could pick the ones with the weakness, give it for free, and then reel them in and watch them flop about at her feet.

By the time I had put my clothes back on and combed my hair, guests were starting to arrive. Ramona was standing in front of Mia, who wore a luxurious satin maid's outfit and had on fishnet stockings and Betty Boop pumps.

"Eyes down," Ramona said sternly, "ass out. Anyone shows interest, refer them to me."

"Yes, madam," was Mia's reply before slipping away.

The guests showing up were definitely gangbangers. I recognized them from the files I'd read on the case. Oddly, their demeanor was as if they were arriving at a literary festival—quiet respect and sobriety, so far anyway. I wondered if Ramona was naturally a part of any gang or if this was a way for the Lone Wolves to keep their eyes on things. Maybe it was Ramona's way of pissing off her uncle. Perhaps it was just a cluster-fuck. Even Ramona probably didn't know.

The first person that caused me to choke on a palm full of cashews was Rachael Lee, Lyle Ng's wife. She was known as a collector of gambling debts, and ruthless at it. Her reputation preceded her, making her job easier. She was thin and relatively shapeless, with narrow hips and unnoticeable breasts, but had on a pair of gorgeous thigh-high leather boots, a perfectly fitted leather dress that laced up the sides and had a rock on her ring finger that looked as though she'd bought it at Bedrock Jewellers. Her face was beautiful, though, in spite of the mask of makeup she wore, and drew in looks from everyone. Her mouth was fixed in an insolent pout. She could put a fork in your eye without blinking.

The file on her told the story of Rachael, at the ripe age of sixteen, beating and kicking the shit out of another teen at a mall while security guards watched. Apparently the security firm's contract forbade them physically intervening, so they stood by while they phoned police. The toe of Lee's boot had nearly blinded the unfortunate victim. After leaving, Lee had come back to dish out more. By the time charges were to be laid, a judge had ruled the videos inconclusive, and in the end, the security guards muffed the line up. Lee had openly laughed at the complainant on the court steps.

Ng himself arrived with Charles O, the Tarantula's main muscle. O was an ancient and rare Chinese name, one that had caused CSIS computers more than a few glitches. O stood 6'4" and had an almond-shaped face and thick, wavy hair slicked back with pomade. He wore a dark grey suit with a purple tie and looked exotic and handsome, with wide shoulders and an almost too narrow waistline. Ng was a smaller man but no doubt the boss. O walked behind and not with Ng, who had bristly hair and glassy, hyperactive eyes that flitted about the room. He wore black slacks and a tight-fitting burgundy silk shirt with a narrow black tie. You could see through the shirt his muscles, which looked like they'd been carved from wood.

I felt a little underdressed without the tie, but my Caballero was expensive and my Ralph Lauren shirt had buttoned down collars and looked sharp. I never wore ties when I knew I might throw down. Once you get a hold of one, lights out.

Ng stood with O, each holding a cup of punch they'd ladled out of a bowl that was infused with dry ice and smoking like a cauldron. Ng pinched his nostrils obsessively: coke addict. I stood to the side, saying hi politely to anyone who passed, sipping on a pale ale with a wedge of lime jammed down the neck. Ng was constantly turning his head, looking here and there, as if someone was about to jump him. Someone was.

14

If you'd accidentally walked into Ramona's party, you'd never have thought from the look of the guests who they were and what they did. Not at first, anyway. However, there was a noxious aura that seemed to fill the room, like smoke in a cigar lounge or slime at a haunting.

Ng seemed friendly enough, but you could see discomfort in the faces of those he spoke with, a mix of fear and uncertainty. After a half hour, I made a point to bump into him at the snack table, where he was piling a plate with candied salmon, to see for myself what he was like.

"How do you know Ramona?" I asked him as I ate a piece of salmon jerky.

"I don't. She knows me," he answered without looking at me.

What do you say to that?

O stood back a bit, hands clasped behind him. He wore expensive cologne and had on several rings meant primarily to indent cheekbones.

Sade's voice powered through the speakers, sounding distant and ephemeral.

"I'm surprised at her choice of music," I said, referring to the utter lack of bar beat, which is what I'd expected after hearing her choice of music on her Web site.

Ng glanced at me blankly and said, "She's not playing the music. She's in the kitchen pouring drinks."

There was no room to respond to Ng's comments. He was one of those contrarians whose every comment is meant to be the last. I imagined it'd be impossible to ever have a normal conversation with the numbskull. I decided to poke the tiger.

"Who's the hottie with the rock of Gibraltar?" I asked, flipping my string of salmon in Rachael's direction.

O stepped forward, his eyes away, his hands clasped, listening.

"No one you'd want to know," Ng replied, his eyes on my breastplate and not my eyes.

"Nice talking with you," I said sarcastically.

I stepped away with a paper plate of salmon jerky and left them, feeling O's eyes on the back of my head. If you weren't born with that skill, you sure learned it fast on a tour in Afghanistan. But I'd learned all I needed to: that there'd be no point in conversation when it came down to cases. They'd understand one thing and one thing only, which was fine by me. I was fluent in that tongue.

In the dining room, which was off the living room and open to the kitchen, a man approached Ramona, who had in her hand a highball half filled with vodka, and spoke into her ear. Ramona stood back and said something to him. He then reached into his pocket and counted into her palm

150 dollars. Ramona tucked the money into her cleavage, walked away, and found her maid, tray in hand, standing near the bar. Ramona had Mia put down the tray, gestured toward the client, then spoke firmly, and punctuated whatever she was saying by pointing a finger in Mia's face, pinching her cheeks roughly and sending her off with a slap to the buttocks. This was a ritual that would repeat a half dozen times before the night was through.

When I put my attention back to the room, Ng was speaking with a newly arrived guest, a man I recognized as his brother, Danny. The file on Danny pegged him as a tougher street fighter who had tried the professional cage but somehow caved under the pressure. He was a gym fighter, though, and obviously lacked the sociopathic tendencies that had made Lyle boss. He was the same height but heavier than Lyle, and was wearing black slacks and a white collared shirt opened to expose a gold chain.

I didn't see the payoff in doing anything here. I was outnumbered, and Ramona's place was too nice to trash. I'd need to pick them off one at a time, or at least get them when there were only two together, perhaps outside going to their car, or maybe I could follow them after the party.

I minded my own business for a while and took a stroll around. The marble counter in the front bathroom was where the coke was lined and snorted, and some moron was walking around selling ecstasy and Viagra. As the night wore on, the party peaked at around fifty people, always someone coming or going. The energy waned, and I could see a need for the Ngs and O to get out and go someplace where there was more action. Besides, between midnight and five was probably when they did most of their trade.

When I saw them gather near the front door, around one in the morning, I got a feeling in my gut not unlike the one a kid gets when his mom comes home with triple chocolate iced cream. I went to look for Ramona, to say good-bye.

She was in an armchair in the corner of her bedroom, her drink held to her lips. Her maid knelt naked in front of her, wrists duct taped behind her back, a strip of duct tape flattened over her mouth. Ramona had one shoe off and her stocking-clad foot pressed to her maid's face. Mia struggled passionately to breathe when Ramona pinched her nostrils with her toes, and Ramona laughed when she released her grip and Mia desperately inhaled her mistress.

Ramona took the money from her cleavage and counted it and said, "You'd love to kiss me, wouldn't you?" With the toe of her stiletto, she stepped on Mia's gas.

I left that unforgettable scene and followed the goons out the door, not so close though that they'd see me. Lyle Ng and his wife Rachael got in the back, and O got into the driver's side of a charcoal BMW 735i. I didn't see where Danny had gone. I ran through some hedges to the Skyline, which was just around the corner, and hopped in. The BMW had already headed south on Lonsdale, but I fired up the ignition and was ten car lengths behind them in 3.5 seconds. I hit the toggle to drop the whale tail, to be less conspicuous.

I took my right hand off the shifter and felt the cold metal corkscrew in my leather jacket pocket. The suppressed Sig Mosquito was affixed under the dash.

"Hang on to your fucking hats," I said.

15

If you're going to buy or even borrow a car with more than 500 hp, you need to take a drifting course, to learn how your car handles, to learn how to drift it so that you don't kill yourself or anyone else when you inevitably hit a corner too fast. I'd taken the course, in Germany, and knew O likely hadn't, so there was no chance he'd lose me even if they saw me following them. The Beemer had tinted windows and was impossible to see into, but at night, they'd have a harder time seeing me, too.

They headed to the notorious downtown Eastside, Canada's most desolate urban strip, where they made two conspicuous stops, Ng talking with crack whores both times, with nothing exchanging hands. What happened next I couldn't have scripted better. O circled the block, looking for an address on Abbott, but had to drop off Ng and his wife and park around the corner, on Pender, where he waited in the car. I parked halfway down the street, got out of the Skyline, and looked both ways before crossing the street. Traffic was dead.

When I was about twenty feet from the Beemer, I picked up a stone and threw it as hard as I could at the back window. I began to jog toward the driver's side door as O opened it to get out.

A glint caught my eye. O had a gun in his left hand, but as he stepped out, he was standing up and pivoting on his left foot, and I caught him off balance. I kicked his left forearm against the car door, which I now noticed was armored. The thick, heavy door didn't budge, and O let out a howl and bull-rushed his way onto the sidewalk to face me squarely.

Adrenaline raced through my veins. I needed this like right-wing conservatives needed hate. I leant back and watched a left jab and a straight right miss by a mile, and then leapt in with a knee to the liver that I followed through to tomorrow. O buckled and went down. I wasted no time getting the corkscrew out, planting it into his shoulder just above where the pec inserts. As I centred all my weight on his chest, I twisted the corkscrew into him.

He let out a howl that would have made a wolf run away with its tail between its legs. I postured up and popped him twice on the jawbone, putting him out. I twisted the corkscrew all the way in, took out his wallet, put it in my pocket, and left him and then stood up and looked around me, hoping no one was recording this with a fucking cell phone. One shadowy figure down the street had stopped to look, but then turned and kept on. I glanced at the gun, thought about it, and then decided to leave it. If the cops came, they could get him for that and the armored car, which were both illegal in this country.

I turned the corner onto Abbott and had lost track of what door the lovely couple had gone into. When I stopped and turned to recalculate, the Ngs stepped from a dark entryway. Ng was so surprised to see me he looked as if he'd hit an invisible wall, and looking into his calculating eyes, I could smell the smoke from his liquor-cooled micro-processor overheating. I punched Rachael first, thinking all the while about the dreadful things she had done that were itemized in her file on my netbook.

Ng drove his fist at me and connected, flush, but he was a lightweight. I'd been hit harder by Ramona. I front-kicked him on his breastplate, stepped back while he stumbled on the curb, and swung a high roundhouse kick he tried block-ing with his arms. He fell straight to the sidewalk like a felled tree. His eyes were open, but there was no calculat-ing going on.

I stumbled over Ng's wife to finish him, and he actually let out a squeal when I fired the toe of my shoe into his floater rib. He brought down his arms to protect his mid-section, and I flattened his nose with one, perfectly timed foot stomp.

Ng was still conscious—I'll give him that—but he was wishing he wasn't. Blood gushed out his nose and down his throat, causing him to choke. Rachael was out like a trout, a small stream of red dribbling from her nose and down her cheek. It looked good on her.

Two young gay men stepped from a basement bar and looked over, the expressions on their contented faces show-ing no surprise. This was Abbott Street after all.

I twisted the lapels of Ng's jacket into my fists, lifted him up, and prized him into a recessed doorway that had been cinder blocked shut, and whispered into his semi-conscious brain:

"Mind your little fucking fiefdom, fuck face." There's nothing like alliteration to put fear into the mind of a man. "Fuck with us and you won't have to kill each other in your little war. We'll do it for you."

"W-who t-the fuck are you?"

"You can't see me, little man. I'm in a different dimension. You're a dot—I'm a sphere. I see you at all times. I can reach into you and rip out your fucking lungs without you even knowing it. Hear me?"

He was too fucking proud to bow. I pressed myself in and put him in a standing arm triangle, cutting off the blood in stages, and then releasing him back into consciousness.

"Do you fucking understand?" I whispered.

"Y-y-yes," he said, breathing the words into my ears.

"See, was that so hard?"

I released the choke and leaned back, my hands on his shoulders. He was woozy and might not have stood up on his own steam.

"Charles…" he managed to say.

"O? He can't help. I took care of him earlier. Just remember this, little man: the next time you see me or Marty or Marc, show respect, like any peon would to his master."

Despite the beating and humiliation, it was only then that defeat washed over his eyes, eyes that were used to dishing out his unique brand of sadism, whether it was passing out drugs near playgrounds or accompanying his wife when she put the fear of God into a single mother with a gambling addiction.

In the distance a siren wailed. It was time to fuck off. I let go of Ng, and miraculously he stood on his own. Rachael began to stir. I left the opposite way I'd come, circled the block, and when I got in my car, I backed into Beatty behind me and left without the cruiser seeing me as he drove up Abbott.

I got home around three in the morning and checked myself in the mirror. Not a scratch. Using some smooth Alberta Springs, I made an old-fashioned and stood in the dark while looking out the windows at the lights across the river, which seemed to glint like sunlight off rippled water. As the cool, refreshing drink tried valiantly to do its job, fear washed over me. It wasn't fear of the Ngs or O or Marty or Marc or Vincent, and it wasn't the fear of the injury and pain. As I stood there, a mere flit of a thought of Ramona came into my mind, and instantly I had an erection that was three-quarter cement, one-quarter semen. As visions of her flawless physical beauty came over me, my heart pounded, harder and harder, till I thought my chest would explode. Compulsions that powerful can make you dead very quick. It took every fiber of my will to keep from getting in my car and racing over there. *God help you* was right.

16

I woke at ten and remembered with an electric jolt that I had to be in Steveston by one to train with Pop. It was one of those rare days when I got out of bed and made it to the bathroom and stood in front of the mirror before I realized I didn't have any pain, on a day when there was reason. I made myself a power shake with pea protein powder and mixed berries, stretched on my living room rug, and then threw on a black Adidas warm-up suit trimmed in lime green and made it out the door around noon and went for a jaunt around the block before I got in my car.

It was overcast today with a few breaks in the clouds near Mount Baker, which melded with the sky and appeared like a distant mirage. The air was cool near the river but smelled like locomotive diesel fumes. Even though I didn't have a day job, it felt like Saturday. There was enough traffic, but there were far fewer frantic drivers and not as many horns honking.

I got to my car and checked it over for scratches and rock chips. There were none. I got in and started the engine and roared out to the exit ramp, the squealing tires echoing in the underground and startling a young couple getting into their Mercedes SUV. With food in my gullet, a bottle on the bar, and the Skyline caressing me like Ramona's dress hugged her ass, I was for a second as contented as I could be, touch wood. I looked forward to seeing Pop.

I had no beef with Pop. He was and had been a good father, especially when his wife had absconded, and he was 85 percent responsible for the level of my martial arts training, for the fact that it was a lifestyle more than a sport or activity. But Pop was from another time and place, another era, and I found it hard to relate to his way of thinking: he was very patriarchal. He and Ramona would not get along, I thought, laughing, not that I planned to ever introduce them. He was a loving man but stoic and fairly uncommunicative. He believed actions spoke louder than words. That may be true with some things, but certain dimensions of life deserve a word or two now and again.

Pop's newly constructed two-story, three-bedroom home was not far from the river. I parked on the street down the block a bit and went around to the laneway, where he had a double garage converted into a home gym. The upper level, which in his neighbor's homes were suites, had mats and bars for doing things like pull-ups, push-ups, isometrics, and a selection of resistance bands for strengthening. He'd never lifted weights and didn't believe in them. He felt they stiffened and slowed the muscles.

"Once you're big enough to hurt, it's all technique and gas," he'd say.

He'd never been a mixed martial artist in modern terms. Though he knew karate and catch wrestling, his emphasis had been karate. He was the one who'd taught me the footwork and the kind of discipline to keep distance that had made the difference in my game. He was a smaller man and in his competitions liked to keep away before striking and then falling back, like a cobra, which was his nickname, in fact. His stance was crucial to this tactic, which I'd adopted when I melded his karate with the catch wrestling I loved so much. I loved being able to attack from the outside and then brutalize my opponent from inside, with unconventional throws and locks.

"Hey, Pop," I said when I stepped in through the back door. It was five to one. He was standing in front of a mirror working on his lateral movement.

"Moving left, away from an opponent's power, is something many fighters do not practice enough," he said through labored breath.

Pop was 5'9" and 165 pounds. He'd turned fifty-five this year but only recently showed it. His stringy muscles had begun to get that "old man" look, and his abs sagged a bit in spite of his daily workouts. He wore a pair of black fight shorts I'd bought for him online.

I took off my warm up suit and readjusted my own fight shorts, then went upstairs with Pop, and performed set progressions with all the different exercises his equipment allowed, and then worked on pushing a 150 lb. sandbag across the floor in cycles of twenty seconds on/ten seconds off, for ten minutes. I made it to the corner and vomited into a banged-up metal bucket that had a stencilled

Hello Kitty on the side, wiped my mouth on my sleeve, and went over to Pop.

I'd become a better striker than Pop by the time I was twenty-two, but like many people, Pop was a far better instructor than practitioner. He supervised footwork drills, hand-speed drills, and spent time with me to remove some minor telegraphing of my right hand that had been plaguing me since my accident recovery. He held the mitts and showed me a straight-right, left-hook, right uppercut combo with precise angles that I couldn't wait to try out for real.

After our workout Pop made us a salmon dinner with sticky rice and steamed vegetables. He split what was left of a bottle of white wine that he had in the door of his fridge, one he'd purchased at a local winery.

"Let's see this new car of yours," he said after we'd cleared the table and filled the dishwasher.

"It's not new, new. It's new to me."

I didn't know my dad was into cars. He'd driven blue or tan Hondas his whole life. We went outside just as the light began to fade. The Skyline was three doors down and glowed even in that dimming light. Pop walked around the car, his mouth open but no words coming out. His close-set, compact dark eyes blinked.

"It's a Nissan?" he asked. "I've never seen one of these. When you said Skyline, I thought 'Buick.'"

"They didn't sell these in North America, Pop," I said. "The new version that they sell here is the GT-R. I just like the Skyline better. They have perfect lines. This isn't stock, by the way. It was built at a California tuner."

He put his hand on my shoulder. The stretched, animated facial muscles showed a happy, proud man. They had to: he'd never say it. If he wondered how much it had cost or where I'd gotten the money, he kept that to himself, too. It had never occurred to me to purposefully do anything to make Pop proud of me, but standing next to him, my arm around his shoulders, seeing how happy it made him uplifted me. My life had nearly gone down the tubes, and Pop had been there, had fought with the military about my care, had said to one commander, "He fights for his country, and you let him suffer like that? Shame on you!" I think Pop knew I'd come close to flipping my own switch. He'd suffered with me, even though he'd never mentioned that either.

But if I've learned anything in life, it's that there is no line you can cross where life is perfect, where you are happy ever after. Anything can happen, and often does. The only thing that never changes is that everything always changes. But after two years being rag-dolled by life's waves crashing on my head, I finally had a roller under my feet. Problem was, I could feel the sharks in the water all around me.

17

When I got home from spending the day with Pop, I turned on my cell. I often kept it off or where I couldn't see or hear it because electronic beeps take priority over everything else in this high-tech world—my greatest pet peeve. Zoning it out was the only thing that worked for me.

There was a message from Marty to meet with him at his place late Monday morning. It was an order, not a request.

I was in a groove: the pain was under control, I was training again and in good form, my muscles felt healthy from my intense workouts, and I was sleeping better in spite of my new line of work, which had the potential to keep me up at night.

By the time I reached Marty's acreage in Surrey, it was near noon. A bone white Rolls Royce Phantom sat resplendent in a ray of God light that spotlighted the driveway. I parked behind it. I could see my whole reflection in the Phantom's piano finish. The chromium Spirit of Ecstasy hood ornament and Pantheon grill sparkled in their perfection, but the Skyline did not whimper behind it. I went around to the other side of the house and let myself in through the sliding glass doors.

"Down here," Marty yelled from the basement.

The basement had been locked during the barbeque, and when I got downstairs, I could see why. Unlike the unkempt, messy main floor, the basement was the ultimate man cave. The entire far wall was glass—a shark tank. These were not great whites but sharks nonetheless. I'd never heard of a tank like that in someone's home. An HDTV the size of the side of a van took up most of the opposite wall. Signed and framed hockey and football jerseys surrounded the room. The basement footprint seemed a lot bigger than the upper floors.

"I know," Marty said, watching the dumbfounded look on my face. "Cool, huh?"

He was standing beside a granite-topped wet bar, looking spiffy in a long-sleeved khaki safari shirt. Vincent stood beside him wearing a white dress shirt and blue blazer, no tie, like he was about to board a boat. His bear claw was draped over it all as if to embody the ferocity of a silver-tipped grizzly. Both men looked upbeat, a far cry from how either had looked the last time I'd seen them. That's the problem with individuals whose brains are frying: you never know what to expect them to say or do. This typically has the effect of causing certain personality types to scramble to please them. Not me.

Vincent lifted a highball filled with rum and guzzled.

"Want a drink?" Marty asked.

"Surprise me," I said.

He looked behind him and grabbed a bottle of Cabo Wabo tequila that was shaped like a Jeannie bottle. He poured roughly three ounces into a lowball glass and handed it to me, and then poured one for himself.

I sipped and said, "Wow. That's as good as any whiskey I've had."

"Better be. Three hundred clams for this bottle."

Vincent came around the bar and approached me, pulled from his jacket two bound stacks of twenties and fifties, and handed them to me while he sipped his drink, looking into my eyes the whole while.

"Thanks, Griz," I said

"No need to thank me,"Vincent said. "Griz. I like that."

He sat in one of the leather chairs that angled toward the TV. I took a seat on the couch where I could see him and placed the money on the arm and rested my glass on it. Marty joined us and sat on the other end of the sofa.

"That was some job you did Friday night,"Vincent said. No smile, all business.

"Popcorn," I said.

"Popcorn?" Marty asked.

"Easy as making popcorn," I said.

"You've raised eyebrows, Char,"Vincent said.

I looked at him carefully. A pleasant odor, like port-steeped pipe tobacco, emanated from him. Just then he removed a pipe from his inner pocket, stuffed it with tobacco from a thick, plastic pouch, and withdrew a lighter shaped like a pearl-handled snub-nosed .38 and lit the pipe. It was quite the ceremony.

You would never have guessed that this man was president of the Lone Wolves, especially driving his Rolls, but if someone told you, you'd think for a second and say, "Oh K." He didn't seem any more money oriented or socio-pathic than any oil company executive.

"I'm finding the sweet spot," I said. "Most of us change careers five or six times before we hit our stride."

I sipped. The tequila tasted better with each gulp, if that were possible.

"My concern with freelancers, Char, is that they have a tendency to become unwieldy."

"Everyone in this biz is unwieldy," I offered.

His mouth took the shape of a smile, but it wasn't a real smile. Honestly, I'd been more awed by Vulture than by this man, but I didn't underestimate the length and grip of his venomous tentacles. Famous and infamous people alike rarely live up to expectations when you see them in person.

"In degrees. I just want you to hear it from me. You have quickly become a friend of the Wolves and are already a valuable asset. But make no mistake: you are an asset, and as much good as you can do for this organization, you really don't want to fuck with it."

His voice emanated from his cavernous chest like the echo of a door creaking in Dracula's castle. I decided to keep it zipped and let him speak. That's what he was here for, not to listen to anything I had to say.

"If you're going to involve yourself with Ramona," he said, letting out a lungful of smoke and rolling his eyes, "keep in mind that anything you do reflects onto her."

By that he meant that enemies could get to me through hurting her. In other words, a relationship with her affected my work, my value to him. Everything is a mind fuck with these guys, I thought.

I nodded seriously because that's what I thought he'd want to see, and rolled the tequila in the lowball. Ramona could take care of herself, but I didn't say that.

"Any questions?" he said, his brow furrowed.

"What's my next job, Griz?" I asked, patting the cash.

This smile that spread across Vincent's face was real. He gulped down what was left of his drink as if it were Kool-Aid. Marty laughed and slapped my shoulder. When I looked over at Marty, he seemed nervous, though, like he could never be sure how these meetings ended. Always on eggshells.

A momentary, uncomfortable silence got us to our feet. We made our way next to the shark tank, like friends might do. One of the fish hovered in the water, facing us, imposing its toothy face into Vincent's reflection, making it look for a second that the biker had a shark's face, but it swam away with a quick jerk, having lost a staring contest to a more vicious predator.

18

"We have two people taking a truck to Washington State," Marty said, once Vincent had left and we had begun our second tequila. The skin on his face began to glow, although the Mexican liquor didn't seem to make him happier. In fact, the more he drank, the more morose and monotonous his voice became, till it was an effort for him just to drag it up from whatever depths it had fallen. "We need you to go down separately, to act as their guardian angel."

I watched one of the sharks, whose prehistoric and curious shape resembled a modern fighter jet.

"What am I protecting?" I asked.

Marty weighed in his mind how much he should reveal to me. It wasn't enough for me to do dirty deeds dirt cheap. My infiltration had a purpose.

"I'm not going to the States, where their fucking war on drugs nets you life in prison for carrying a roach clip, unless I know what I'm protecting and who."

I wouldn't win any popularity contests with the Lone Wolves by being a total yes-man. I needed to protect myself somehow.

"They're driving an F-350 welding truck with a faux propane tank filled with bud. They're coming back with cocaine. It's a straight trade this time, but worth a lot of money. Some of our contacts south of the border have got a bit hairy lately. The truck is well made. They'll get through the border. It's their liaison I'm concerned about."

Marty polished off his drink and with a shaky hand poured another. This was a man on a fast road to liver failure. Live fast, die obliterated.

"You'll rendezvous with them in Bellingham, at an industrial mall. You'll be in the open at that point. You'll be dealing with some fucked-up head cases from Huntington Beach. My drivers are able to get through the border without breaking a sweat but can't deal with serious muscle. It's precautionary, but..." Marty's voice trailed off into his tequila.

It seemed simple enough to me, but Marty's elusive eyes begged to differ.

"One day's work, five Gs," he added.

The compunctious mask Marty wore was the cover of a book I never wanted to read. Looking at the lines on his face reminded me of *American Psycho*, a book I never wanted to reread. I needed to get away from Marty for fear I'd absorb him through osmosis and be mind fucked forever.

I agreed to the job, which wasn't for a couple of days. I drove home after checking my blood alcohol level on a meter I'd bought for that purpose, and went online and compulsively brought up Ramona's Web site and scrolled through the pages, like I was reading her diary.

The free pages introduced the user to her, with still shots and some of the videos that were on her YouTube page. There were downloadable stills and videos and a bio page that read:

Into: bondage, discipline, foot fetish and worship, online slave training, financial domination, financial ruination, humiliation, expensive gifts.

One of the videos was Ramona taking over someone's computer and spending twelve hundred of his dollars on gifts for herself. A portion of her members were female. This could never have been done pre-Internet and pre-You-Tube. People like Ramona needed to throw their hooks far and wide to catch enough fish to make something like this worth their while.

I needed to know more about who and what I was dealing with. I brought out my credit card and purchased a month's membership for $14.99. This brought me to a much raunchier page with videos she could never have uploaded to YouTube. One fifteen-minute video was entirely of Mia performing oral for Ramona while two unidentified men massaged her feet with their tongues.

I found myself on Ramona's donation page, where you could hit the donate button and direct cash into her personal account or go to her page on Amazon and choose from a list of things she wanted that you could purchase for her. I was astonished to find two pages of gifts that had been bought for her, with many big ticket items, like $350 boots, an iPhone, a laptop, dozens upon dozens of CDs and DVDs.

I tried to work out in my mind how someone got to a point where there was literally no governor on where their mind and soul went, but not before clicking on and purchasing for Ramona a fashionable TapouT warm-up suit for $150. After the purchase, I was led back to a pink screen with Ramona's beautiful face, her lips pursed into a kiss, and below that, *You're Welcome!*

Fitting.

I put my computer to sleep and got out my netbook and updated my files for this job and found the number for Wil Mahood, the more amiable of the two CSIS agents assigned to keep tabs on me. I wrote it down in code onto a slip of paper and slide that into my wallet.

I was just about to head down to the waterfront for a bite to eat when the phone rang.

"Hello."

"Hey, sweetie," Ramona said.

"Ramona, I was just thinking about you."

"Yeah, thanks for the track suit. There's more where that came from, I hope."

This woman was in a strange league all her own. A shiver went down the length of my spine, as if I'd been transfused with liquid nitrogen.

"Come over, now," she said, pleasantly enough. "Bring a nice bottle of wine."

She hung up the phone without waiting for my response. Like a remote controlled car with Ramona at the wheel, I threw on some fresh clothes and drove to the closest liquor store.

19

I didn't know what I expected to find at Ramona's. What I got was a reality check. Ramona wore fashionable designer jeans and an Affliction top that accentuated her athletic back and arms. Her corneas had a glaze to them that pulsated, like the Terminator's. The overwhelming impression I got from her was the one a blackout drunk got when he walked past a bar: insatiable desire mixed with authentic dread. There was pity mixed in, too, rooted in seeing a woman whose innocence had been destroyed and who had been used to such an extent that this was the only relationship she could have with anyone, and pity for a man who'd come to her.

Ramona's was a theme that repeated itself in the Vancouver underworld. Vincent, Marc, Marty, and the Tarantula members I'd met had come from broken homes and abuse, their trajectory skewed at birth. Gang life was their pseudo-family, where they could fit in with people like themselves.

Dinner with Ramona was decent enough, but in the hour and a half I was there, people were coming and going like her condo was a Skytrain station. Her phone only stopped ringing when she gabbed into it. In between, she was constantly checking the computer in her office, from where she ran her operation. She was gregarious, giving her attention to so many that she gave it to no one. Under my breath I dubbed her Miss Piggy.

At around eight o'clock, I'd had enough and let myself out while Ramona was updating her blog. I didn't want to be rude, but she certainly had been. I walked to my car feeling relief. I drove to the River Rock Casino and played blackjack in a room with about ten thousand other oriental men and women and decided to leave my table around eleven, after finding myself up a 140 bucks.

"Paid for the stupid, fucking track suit," I told myself.

On the stairs leading down from the entrance to the slot machines was a sour-faced man in a grey suit and red tie. He was six feet maybe, built like a slag heap, with shoulders that sloped downward from no neck and topping a thick chest. An even larger belly strained his suit coat button. He looked to be in his early thirties.

As I approached the stairs, the big man held my eyes and stepped sideways to block my exit. He reached into his pocket and pulled out a leather fold and opened it. VPD. This wasn't good.

"Step over here, please," he said, indicating a spot near a row of slots.

His head was conical, like his body, with fine blond hair almost like peach fuzz. His skin was blotchy. Behind him, up near the entrance, a bandy-legged man in a blue suit and hoary face watched us but kept his distance. He was so thin his coat hung on him like he was a broom stick. I assumed he was the Lunkhead's partner.

"Can I see some ID?" he asked.

"Nope."

I looked him straight in the eye.

"C'mon, hands against the wall, now," he said, his voice low.

Why would the VPD approach me if they were monitoring me? Wouldn't they want to keep in the shadows till they had something on me? If they were going to approach me, why not in the parking garage, away from people? Why was Broomstick loitering in the background like he was afraid or embarrassed? This didn't feel like an official visit. Every force has members on the take. The possibility occurred to me that Lyle Ng had a friend at police headquarters. I hadn't been doing this shit long enough to have a list of reasons VPD, or anyone, would stop me like this.

"Fuck you, Lunkhead. Go suck an egg," I told him calmly, calling his bluff.

He reached out and took hold of my arm. I tried wrenching it out of his grasp, but he had a grip like a gorilla's, probably from overloading his fork his whole life. We stalemated, our bit of struggle attracting the attention of a few people coming in and going out, but most people were too intent on losing money to care. The security guard was watching and doing nothing. Obviously he'd been schooled by Lunkhead, who patted down my jacket for weapons while we stood face to face. His hand hit the remote for my neurotransmitter. When he reached for it, I isolated his arm, spun, and hip-tossed him to the carpet.

The security guard stepped forward and then halted. I had Lunkhead's arm twisted behind his back and shoved it as far up as I could, not quite breaking it, before I let go and stood back.

Broomstick rushed over and helped up his partner. Guns were not drawn, and I wasn't under arrest, so I'd been right. This was a lame-assed attempt to ensure I was who they thought I was and then to put pressure on me.

Two more security guards came toward the one stationed at the stairs, who spoke with them or waved them off.

"You touch me again, Lunkhead, it'd better be under official VPD business, or I'll knock that fucking block off," I said under my breath. "You too, Broomstick."

"No, you listen here," Lunkhead said. "You're putting your nose where it's gonna get clipped, see. Keep it up and I'll come down on you like an anvil."

He massaged the arm with his free hand and held it stiffly at his side. A hurt look came over him, a weakness in the mouth, the kind of look a kid gives when the wheel snaps off his favorite Tonka Toy and he's about to cry.

"Next time you won't see it coming," Broomstick said, his voice sounding like a rasp filing a chunk of rust, a voice that would have better suited Lunkhead.

"No. Now I'll be waiting for you, asshole."

A feeling had come over me like mist over a graveyard, all the anger that had built since Afghanistan roiling in my brainpan and visible through my retinas. Broomstick stepped back suddenly, a frightened look in his eyes. The only thing that kept me from killing them both that night was the knowledge that the entire ceiling of the casino was studded with fisheye cameras. That and luck, because when the anger swells in me, I am its marionette. Once my blood boiled, I had about as much control over it as I do over this rock hurtling though space.

20

I read somewhere that belief in God, afterlives, and the supernatural may have come from dreams, in which you see relatives and loved ones. Oddly enough, that night I dreamed pleasant dreams. I dreamed of fighting in the UFC—something I knew I'd never do. In my dream, I cleaned out my division.

The reason I knew I'd never compete in MMA is that, as much of a fan as I was, my background was catch wrestling. MMA has rules, plenty of them, and catch wrestling, the kind I'd done since a child, did not. Nor do fist fights in alleys have rules, and that, my friend, changes your mindset entirely. MMA is close to the real thing but not the real thing. I concluded that the work I was doing for CSIS hit the spot big time.

After eating breakfast, I called Mahood.

"Mahood," was how he answered his phone.

"Char here. I need to meet with you today."

He hesitated. I could hear a car horn honking in the background and a locomotive chugging its rhythmic beat as it accelerated. There was a locomotive moving eastward below my condo next to the river. I wondered if Mahood was in New Westminster, keeping his eye on me.

"Okay," he said at last.

"I don't want fuckhead there," I told him, referring to Steroid-freak O'Malley. "Just you. I have enough dickheads on this side of the line."

"No probs," he said. "Meet me at the Tim's in PoCo, the one just down from the Pickton's old farm."

"That turn you on?" I asked.

"Noon," he said, and hung up.

My comment had been uncalled for, and I regretted it for half a second. I'm not sure why I had to drive to hell and back for a ten-minute meeting, but I didn't want to talk on the phone, and I had the day to myself.

I took Lougheed, weaving in and out of traffic that was driving far too slow for my money. A Z7 tried unsuccessfully to beat me off the line as I'd made my way into Coquitlam.

A ramp to the Coast Meridian Overpass had just been built behind the Tim Horton's, and the lot was gravel and still wet and puddled. I drove my car in slowly, avoiding a couple of potholes, pulling beside a metallic blue Lincoln Navigator with tan leather interior. Mahood sat in the driver's seat.

Mahood stepped out of his SUV, looked over my car, and said, "I'll buy you a coffee."

Mahood's hair was flattened to the top of his head, like he had been rained on or had used too much conditioner.

Tim Horton's was full, but we managed two chairs in the corner, near the window, where we could talk without being overheard. I had a large double-double and one of those maple Danishes with nine thousand calories. Mahood had his coffee black, no sugar, no cream, a crueller on the side.

"I have a job in Seattle," I said. "Tomorrow. I'm riding shotgun on a drug run."

"Good to know."

He sipped his coffee with a calm face, looking around him at the crowd clambering for a seat.

"I guess I could've picked a better time to meet here," he said, then looked at me, and told me, "You'll be okay. Any trouble with their feds, we'll get you back."

Honestly, I didn't have much confidence in him or the CSIS. They'd been under a lot of fire recently for mishandling cases of all kinds on foreign soil. The RCMP was also losing face after their Tazerring of Robert Dzekanski and their general inability to own up in a reasonable time frame.

"How much are they paying you?" he asked.

Of course, I wasn't allowed to make anything from the crimes I was committing for the sake of infiltrating the Lone Wolves.

"I'm depositing everything in CSIS's account," I lied.

He nodded but seemed unconcerned. It was a relatively small item on his daily list of things to worry about.

"How far you digging?" he asked.

"Far," I answered, smiling into my cup as I drank. "I think I may have found my calling."

"With us or them?"

"What's the difference?"

He almost answered me but cut himself off.

"One other thing," I said.

He set his cup down, leaned back, and peered into my eyes.

I leaned forward and said, "I had a visit last night... from the VPD."

Mahood's eyes widened, and he leaned into me.

"What kind of visit?" he asked.

"Unofficial, I'd say. They tried strong-arming me at the River Rock. Out of the blue, near the lobby."

"What do you make of it?"

"I'm a bit green but not stupid enough to think official VPD business is conducted this way. They seemed green, unprofessional."

I reached into my pocket and took out a sheet of paper with the descriptions of Lunkhead and Broomstick. Mahood took it in his hands, set it down on the table, and flattened it with his wet palm.

"Tch, tch, tch," clicked from Mahood's mouth, and a look came over him reminiscent not of a principal but of a truant officer reading the file of an absent pupil. A smile slowly crept across his face, and he couldn't have been happier.

"That's why I love this job," he said, finishing his coffee. "You never know what you'll flush."

Outside a woman with the proportions of an award-winning pumpkin and a dress with the color to match stepped from her Corolla and into a pot hole, her whole foot disappearing into the mud. I started laughing from the belly till everyone but Mahood was looking at me. I hadn't laughed like that in a while. When I saw the woman had twisted her ankle, I went out to help her, came in, and bought her order for her and took it out to her. I'm no fucking boy scout, but I had been a soldier for Christ's sake.

21

Going to America always gives my head a proper shake. When you watch TV, you become deluded into thinking everyone there is a rock star, movie idol, or sports hero, and that they're all bathing in tubs of money. The truth is that for every stellar success story there are ten thousand sorry souls bussing tables all day and living in moldy, moss-covered trailers or barren studio apartments, every one of them unwilling to give up this way of life because more than anything they want to be the next Bill Gates and actually believe they might be.

I made it through the border in record time. For every luxury SUV on the highway down there were a hundred jalopies, their fenders dragging sparks along the shoulder. There was unkemptness not just in the cluttered yards but on town and city property alike. It was a dreary day even before the rain started to come down in sheets, reducing visibility to less than a kilometer.

I didn't have far to go. The industrial mall was outside of Bellingham, not far off the highway. I was to wait for the welding truck at a Sunoco station, which I found easily enough, and went in and bought a coffee and asked directions into Seattle, which I wasn't going to, then ran back out to my car, and sat and listened to a CD of Rodrigo, played not with piano but Spanish guitar. My mind went to Clint Eastwood and the spaghetti westerns, where his character never got angry and exploded. The only way you knew Blondie was ready to go was the cigarillo in his mouth moved from one side to the other, a mentality I strove to emulate.

I saw the welding truck emerge from a cloud of rain and rumble down the highway toward me, lopsided and looking as though it were askew and moving at a slight angle. The truck pulled into the gas station and two men in denim pants and jackets—not exactly rain gear—got out and went into the store and came out with Dr. Peppers and glanced knowingly at me and sat in their truck. Then the driver got out and came over to me. I opened the passenger door, and the man got in.

He was average in every way and had a three-day beard and workingman's hands. He smelled like propane, though his clothes were clean. His brown hair was curly and mid-length. He and his partner looked like what they were purporting to be: welders going to work.

"You're the point man," he said.

He fumbled for a pack of cigarettes, got one out, stuck it on his bottom lip, but didn't bother looking for a match.

I nodded. "Char."

"Nice to meet you, Char. I'm Ted. That there is Doug," he said, pointing toward his partner. "Here's the deal: We need you to come in with us and take care of any horseshit.

These fuckers are fucked, in the head. Real head cases, man. That all began when we started bringing coke and heroin back instead of cash. Julio and Junior are two bangers from Huntington. It's not our specialty. Our specialty is getting the shipment down and back safely. Can you handle it?"

"We'll find out," I said.

He looked at me suspiciously, but I winked and lifted my sippy cup to my lips.

It was my intent to deprive these lowlifes information about me or how I felt. What would be the point in letting them in?

Ted stared through the windscreen, mesmerized by the water sluicing downward. He looked at his watch and said, "We're on in twenty. Maybe head over and watch who comes in, then come to the bay door when you see us pull up."

That sounded fine to me, but I'd do whatever I felt I had to on this job.

"What have you got for firepower?"

"Exactly what I'll need," I said. It's better to keep them in the dark.

We looked at each other, and I swear I could smell death, like it had soaked into his jacket. I'd had that feeling in Afghanistan, the knowledge that the man you're standing next to is on borrowed time. He was a normal-looking man in every way, but looking into his denuded eyes, I could smell his demise.

He got out of my car without saying anything more and walked over to the welding truck. I started the Skyline, put it into gear, and headed over to the industrial park. I found the address and then spun around and parked amongst a row of cars facing the highway and away from the buildings, in an adjacent lot, out of view of any surveillance cameras.

The light was fading, and the rain was so hard a foggy mist seeped out of the earth.

I couldn't have missed the Huntington Beach badasses. They pulled into the lot five minutes after I did, driving a maroon Volvo SUV without tinted glass. Seeing their mugs drew me back, like looking into a baby carriage and seeing a rabid Rottweiler staring back at you.

When the Volvo had gone around the corner, I got out, opened the trunk, popped the lid to my secret compartment, and looked down at my pride and joy. They didn't stand a chance.

22

Julio and Junior were large men of Mexican descent who carried their weight like bats. Even in the inclement weather, both men wore wife-beater shirts and bore tattoos, many of them rough prison tatts. Both men wore Mexican flag tattoos on their shoulder. They looked like demented Klingons. It evaded me how these two could get away with anything, let alone transporting drugs in a vehicle on a main highway. Their faces in that Volvo SUV had "pull me over" written all over them.

I got out the M10 and shoved it into a strap I'd sewn into my Caballero and, when I looked at myself in the reflection of the window of the Skyline, couldn't tell I was packing even a lone cigarette. The welding truck pulled into the lot and went around back. I followed, a ball cap tugged down tight over my head to keep off the rain.

The M10 is a thing of beauty. With it, you can chop down a hemlock in about thirty seconds, one of the big ones, not a sapling. They shoot so many rounds/second, you could vaporize small animals with it, if you wanted. I was feeling the power when I turned the corner and saw the tail end of Ted enter the bay door, hands up, one of the Mexican thugs driving the SUV in behind the welding truck.

I picked up my pace, the whoosh of the pouring rain masking my footfalls. I could see the meaty forearm of one of the Mexicans pull on the chain to bring the door down. I scooted noiselessly under it, the M10 drawn.

The one closest to me pulled a Glock and fired it at my midsection. The bullet stood as much of a chance against the Caballero as a mosquito did trying to pierce sheet metal. Tourists in Bogota actually go to Caballero's shop to experience being shot.

The one who'd tried plugging me expected me to go down. Everyone in the room expected me to go down. I brought the M10 down on the neck of the one who'd fired from close range and watched his load observe the law of gravity. His gun clattered on the cement at my feet, which I kicked behind me.

Luckily, the other Mexican was on the far side of the room. He pulled a nickel-plated .44 on Ted. The one nearest me groaned in agony and rubbed his neck and shoulder. I tugged on the chain and finished closing the door while aiming the M10 at the other Beano.

The only thing worse than looking down the barrel of a .44, is seeing someone waving an M10. There is no chance for anything in its path.

Julio, who was lying at my feet, had *Julio* tattooed in script on his left deltoid, which I noticed only now.

"Drop the gun, Junior. I'll mow down everything in the room, including you," I said to Ted.

Ted's face showed a mix of relief and fear. He was glad I'd shown up but wasn't sure about me anymore.

The bay was a cement box with a set of rough pine stairs leading up to the semblance of an office, where there was a computer and a few filing cabinets yellowing under an incandescent bulb. Behind Junior, there was a door to a washroom partially propped open.

All eyes were on the M10 as I screwed onto it an aluminum silencer. Overtop of the fluorescent buzz, I could hear the Mexicans swallow. I'd decided during the drive down that the only way to do a job like this was with brute force. That's what had worked for Vincent, and it's what had worked for the Mexicans' boss. That's the language of the business, and I'd make it work for me.

Junior dropped his gun to the cement floor with a metallic thud that echoed throughout the room.

Julio's eyes wavered.

"Turn around," I said to him.

He hesitated and then shuffled around slowly. In his belt was another .44.

"Take it out and drop it to the floor," I told him.

He obeyed, but I could see the tension of his thick neck muscles as he gritted his teeth.

"Okay," I said, since none of them had enough saliva to form words in their mouths, "Julio and Ted, over there. Doug and Junior, finish off the trade."

Ted and Junior went to the back corner where I could keep an eye on everyone. Doug took out his toolbox and began dismantling the wire-mesh cage surrounding the faux-propane tank. He then began removing faceplates on the bottom of the passenger-side doors. In thirty minutes, the exchange had been made, and both vehicles reassembled in another thirty.

When we were ready to go, I said, "Tell your boss to send up someone more capable. Now get in the Volvo and get the fuck out."

The Mexicans got in the SUV and backed out as I raised the door, and then Ted and Doug followed. I winked at Ted, who gave me a high five, but his face looked devoid of blood. When they'd all left, I gathered up the guns and closed the door, and with a careful scan of the lot and field beyond, I went around the building, opposite from the way I'd come. I didn't have room for the .44s, so I dropped them down a sewer grate a few kilometers down the highway after polishing them down with a rag.

Some of my fellow soldiers liked to listen to rap or heavy metal before going out on a tour, to motivate them. By accident I'd found Rodrigo, which had really done the job. And the job had been popcorn, or so I thought, till I woke up two days later and saw a headline on my Yahoo page with this story:

Two men were gunned down in Bellingham yesterday. A maroon Volvo SUV with California plates was parked in a residential area when a woman walking her dog passed by and glanced in the window. The names of the men have not been released.

Panic went through my veins like a jolt of electricity. Had my car been seen in the area? Were there surveillance cameras I couldn't see? That's the problem with having a unique ride. I could always rent a car the next time or buy a used car for certain jobs.

"Nah," I said, pouring a cup of coffee to have with breakfast.

Like an addict who just needs more, I loved walking the edge.

23

Standing at the edge of the Lone Wolves' party in Langley township, I couldn't help but think, "Geez, this is what it must be like when the inmates of the Riverview Insane Asylum get into the liquor cabinet."

When Ramona walked over from her Hummer, the song blasting over the stereo was Depeche Mode's "Corrupt." Perfect:

> I could corrupt you
> It would be easy
> Watching you suffer
> Girl, it would please me
> But I wouldn't touch you
> With my little finger
> I know it would crush you
> My memory would linger
> You'd be crying out in pain
> Begging me to play my games

Ramona even walked to the rhythm of the song and looked straight at me through the blackness and smiled deviously. She wore a brown leather jacket and matching laced ankle boots, and jeans so tight I had to feel them to see of they were painted on. Her hair was tousled, her face tan and beautiful. The woman had a gift. Exactly what it was hadn't yet occurred to me.

The whole party was outside amongst several outbuildings and rows of trees and hedges, on an L-shaped plot at least three kilometers from the next lot, which was a horse ranch surrounded by a white fence. I'd even passed a winery on my way in. A large brick structure had the bar and dance floor, complete with a disco ball the size of a Yugo, but no one was inside. It was a starlit night, a warm breeze coming from the southwest, and there was a pile of wood waiting to be lit.

There were at least a dozen patched members milling about, all drinking excessively but seemingly sober. The one that had "trouble" written across his forehead was a five-foot-five Irishman wearing a green rugby shirt under his patched leather. He was solid muscle built entirely of small-man syndrome.

Ramona came over after getting a tequila sunrise from the bar and stood beside me without saying anything at first.

"Care to dance?" I asked.

She looked at me as if I'd stepped off of a spaceship.

"Where'd you go the other night? One minute you're there, the next you're gone."

"Right back at you," I said.

I sipped my tonic and lime. I wanted to be sober for this.

She looked at me sideways.

"Who's the runt?" I asked while she was looking at the Irishman.

Ramona shook her head, sipped her drink, and said, "That's Kerwin. You do not want to fuck with him. Not even you, Char. The man's a complete nut job. Vincent used to use him for the kind of work you do, till he realized Kerwin liked it too much. So much that he'd probably do it for free, which is what made it so tough for Vincent to yank his chain."

"Sounds like a dare," I said.

She shook her head emphatically.

"Sounds like a double dare."

Ramona smelled like the air between a whore house and a bubble-gum factory. She leaned forward and kissed me, on the lips, holding my chin with her free hand and turning me away when she was done.

"That's why I need you, Ramona," I said, smiling. "After kicking the shit out of these fucking losers, I feel guilty and need someone's strong hand to discipline me."

Ramona turned her head and peered at me through the dim light, saw the smirk on my face, and left me with a "Cheers!"

Watching all the fuckups, I thought of a good name for this place: Knob Hill Farm.

I kept refreshing my tonic and lime, hoping no one was noticing I wasn't getting loaded or high. As the night wore on, so did Kerwin, strutting around with his chest out, intimidating people he knew would never man-up. You can't win: if you lose, you've lost to a runt, and if you win, you've beat down a runt. He'd always have something to prove. After an hour, other Lone Wolves avoided him, but you could tell they were used to the antics.

Vincent approached the large pit dug out of the ground and ceremoniously lit the bonfire. Three Lone Wolves brought out benches and placed them around the pit. Tonight was a good night to send a message, I thought. Everyone was there to read it.

I made sure to time a trip to the bar when Kerwin was there alone. A few people were dancing under the disco ball, and two women were doling out the liquor, but almost everyone was standing by the fire, its flames licking twelve feet up, the embers drifting off and looking like stars. Kerwin ordered a rye and coke. I sidled up.

"What're ya bruising your whiskey for?" I asked him, my eyes on the barmaid.

"What?" he asked.

I could feel his eyes on me.

"You heard me, little man."

"What the fuck?" he asked again.

"Stella, please," I told the barmaid, then turned, and said, "You heard me, Kermit."

He came at me with the uncontrollable and ferocious intensity of a tornado, wildly throwing haymakers and spinning, off balance, looking like the Tasmanian Devil, sounding like him too. Spittle flew off in all directions, like a lawn sprinkler. I leaned back, hands down, used my feet to keep my distance. He jumped at me and threw a jab followed by a right hook that missed by three feet. I moved left and hit him with a straight right to the jaw, dropping him to the concrete pad.

The music played on, and a crowd quickly gathered outside the outbuilding, the fire to their backs. I took off my Caballero and threw it on the bar top. Kermit got up, felt a drop of blood on his lip, and went ballistic, all rage and aggression, a frightening street brawler but with no real practiced skill: no timing, no distance. He swung a wild left and lifted his right leg up. I swept it from under him and watched him drop again.

I looked over at Ramona and shrugged. She stood next to her uncle, both of them staring at me with eyes that looked like cold, wet gravel. Kermit got up and rushed me. I timed a knee to his skullcap. It was either that or his head plummeting to the cement that put him out. A thin stream of blood spiraled away from under him on the uneven concrete as he lay face down.

No one came to help him, which wasn't a shocker. I put on my jacket and walked over to Vincent and Ramona. The big man spit a stream of tobacco juice to the soil while keeping his eyes on mine and fingering his claw.

I cocked my thumb toward Kermit and said, "Hey, Griz. Time for a change of guard."

Vincent started to laugh, a laugh that had the sound and rhythm of a pile driver. Ramona took my beer, walked over to Kermit, and emptied the bottle onto his head. Finally he began to stir.

"You'll have to watch your back now," Vincent said gravely.

"Maybe I'll just break his."

Vincent regarded me icily, as if I was the crazy fucker.

24

I got home from the party around two in the morning but couldn't fall asleep. I took some prescription anti-inflammatory drugs and washed them down with a highball of single malt, which I finished in large gulps. It's tough watching people drink all night.

I sat in my living room, lights off, letting my eyes glaze over as I stared out the window to the glimmers across the valley reflecting on the river.

There was a chance the heroin I'd helped bring into this country was from Afghanistan, but probably it came from Columbia via Mexico. I didn't have much problem with that. People in these parts of the world needed some kind of income. It had never seemed right to me to wipe out poppy crops to keep the Taliban from turning a profit. We need morphine, and all that accomplished was to alienate the locals. That was the drug war in a nutshell: political, ideological, reactionary, and irrational. Juarez was a war zone now and reflected not the drug trade but free trade, which impoverished millions so a few could stay rich. The new flow I was seeking was supposedly from the Golden Triangle.

Drugs weren't a moral problem for me, and it didn't bother me that I would have to do illegal things to infiltrate the gang culture. Hell, the CSIS expected it of me. But I took issue with the prostitution and human trafficking that gangs like the Lone Wolves get away with, even in countries like Canada.

At the party, I'd overheard a conversation between Vincent, Marty, and the property owner, a weasel of a man named Ronald Watts, regarding their crop of young women on Craigslist. When Johns ordered a girl online, there were almost always pimps involved, especially if the faces in the girls were blurred. Teens are often feuding with their parents or running from abuse. These vulnerable girls become victims to the worst kind of violations. It is impossible for a girl or young woman to battle the organization and the vicious violence criminal gangs offer.

I needed to know how to respond to a potential request to provide muscle against these girls. If Vincent ever did ask me, I just might kill him on the spot. This might not be such a bad option. If I just started whacking these fuck heads, first from one gang, and then the other, who'd know it was me? Everyone would think it was a gang war, just an escalation of the ongoing battle for turf. This idea got me up and over to the bar again, where I poured another glass of single malt.

At three thirty, Ramona called.

"Where are you?" she asked. "Did you leave the party?"

"Yeah, I had enough. I'm at home."

My lips weren't following orders, and my speech was more slurred than Ramona's. She actually sounded sober.

"I'm coming over," she said. "Where do you live?"

My gab should have slammed shut, but the liquor had oiled them up. I gave her directions to where I lived and told her where the New West car park was located.

Being an adrenaline junkie meant not resisting Ramona when she strutted into my condo and dragged me to my bedroom and began kissing me and pulling off my shirt and undoing my pants. It wasn't so much whiskey-dick I was suffering from as Ramona-dick. When she had me flattened on the bed, she secured my wrists to the posts but left my ankles free, and then she stripped in front of me. It was impossible not to watch. Her breasts were fabulously formed and milky white. Her stomach was a washboard, and when she bent to pull off her boots, she revealed the most perfect Japanimation ass I had ever seen. She took off her jeans and peeled off her stockings and shoved those and her panties in my mouth before hopping on. My erection felt like it was made of tempered steel.

I wanted it to never end. The best part was not knowing what this crazy bitch was capable of with me helpless in my own home. I knew that thrilled her. I could feel it in her sway as she rocked herself rhythmically, a smile on her gorgeous face that was nowhere near loving.

"The big, tough guy, sucking on my panties," Ramona said through her breath. I almost couldn't hear her, as though the breeze outside had wrought her words.

When she was done with that side of me, she rose up, pulled the stockings and panties from my mouth, spun herself around, and smothered me unmercifully.

"You may not be able to breathe," she said, a firm grasp on my balls, "but what a way to go, hey?"

When she finished it was because she was exhausted, not because she'd done cumming. She went to sleep beside me, unfastening none of the restraints.

I slept fitfully and had been awake for an hour when Ramona woke and made her way to the shower, glaring at me as she went. I watched in silence as she dried herself next to the bed, not a word coming from her lips, her eyes raking my body now and again. She dressed and went out of the bedroom, and I could hear her in the kitchen making breakfast. When she came back into the bedroom, she sat on the edge of the bed, a plate of eggs and toast and bacon in her hands. She looked down and said, "Boy, you really are enjoying this," and placed the hot plate on my stomach and ate ravenously.

I was mute.

When Ramona was done eating, she left the plate where it was, rising and falling with my breath, and went into the bathroom. I cranked my neck and could see her putting on lip gloss and fixing her hair. She pulled on her boots and put on her jacket and laughed, but not at me.

"I'll tell you what," she said, her face beaming. She went over to my closet, rooted through my jacket, and got my wallet. She opened it, took out everything in it, and threw all but the money on the dresser, sat on the corner of the bed, and counted it in front of me, including the change.

"Two-eighty-six seventy-five. Not much, but it'll do for now."

She put it all in her purse and stood and leaned over me to untie the wrist restraints.

"We'll see what kind of G-force you can withstand," she said as she was leaving. "In the meantime, dream of me."

I could hear her boots clack on the hardwood floor all the way to the front door.

25

Guilt overwhelmed me while I showered. I'm not sure if it was a result of straying from my job or from allowing myself pleasure. While I shaved, I had a difficult time looking into my own eyes. Who was I really? I was starting to lose myself in Ramona, which was a little like watching yourself in a mirror shoot-up for the first time.

I made myself bacon and eggs and waffles smothered in maple syrup and ate while silently staring at my plate. I had to admit to myself that Ramona worked far better than any drug, and even had one up on the neurotransmitter.

I decided I needed to get my head out of the job. Even workaholics take a day off now and then. If I didn't keep my sanity, by visiting Pop or by taking off, I ran the risk of falling too deeply into the life, no matter who was signing my checks.

I got on the Trans Canada, turned on my radar detector, and went about 140km/h till my turnoff. It was a beautiful, sunny day, the sky a light shade of blue, like bone. As I drove along Ninety-sixth, farmland and beautiful houses lining the way, the river not visible but knowable over the rise, I couldn't help but sense that the road was coming to me, not the other way around. It was a perception I'd had on patrol in Afghanistan: that even though we think we choose our way, the reality is that the videogame moves around us. The perception instilled a deep sense of comfort, not unlike being trussed by Ramona.

I felt a million miles from home sitting on a patio in Fort Langley, drinking a straight coffee—no mocha this or latte that—in a cafe on Mavis, next to the courtyard. I went for a stroll through the antique market and found two immaculate 1940s corkscrews, one with a reclined naked woman for a handle. I paid for them at the cash-out, and when I went out into the yellow afternoon light, I felt a wave of panic overtake me. At the corner of Mavis and Glover, a man stepped into a cafe/bookstore called Wendel's. Had he been checking me out?

I didn't have any weapons with me. I went back to the antique market and walked aimlessly, trying to decipher my fear. Ever since I'd gotten back from Afghanistan, I had been hyperaware and paranoid. I wasn't as bad as some of my comrades, whom I loosely kept in touch with, because the first two years home were spent in and out of a hospital bed, in excruciating agony: there had been no time to think I could be shot at.

In my new line of work, it was beneficial to be ultra-sensitive. Paranoia can be a good thing, but it didn't feel good. I began to sense mortar rounds sighting the antique market. I peered suspiciously into stalls that had nothing in them but piles of old wares. I went to the front, to a collection of mahogany carvings of planes, boats, and a '68 Mustang. I partially hid behind a shelf and kept an eye on the window and stepped around to see if I could watch the bookstore entrance. I couldn't see it from there.

Where had I parked my car? My mind began smoking like a burning building and inched toward flashover. Could I get to the Skyline from the side streets? I didn't have my fucking gun with me.

"Can I help you?"

The old man who had taken my money for the cork-screws was standing several feet away from me, hands clenched in front of him. His suspenders kept his pants high above his rotund belly. He looked me up and down, his face a mix of fear and compassion.

I realized then how fast I was breathing. I was hyperventilating.

"I-I'm okay. Thanks," I said, my chest heaving.

I concentrated on my exhalations, tried to let my mind relax, like Pop had taught me. Fear, like desire, overtook me like groundswell hitting a beach, each time the beat and power unpredictable—all of it coming at me. Surf can wear away granite.

If I didn't get out of the market, someone would prob-ably call the police.

"I'm asthmatic," I said, lying. "I need to get outside."

I went to the door and looked to my right, to Wendel's: no one. I walked down Glover and then went over to St. Andrew and found my car as I'd left it. My relaxing day at Fort Langley was over before it had really started.

I spun the tires and headed for Wendel's. The man I'd seen go inside came out just as I parked across the street, next to the railway station. He was with a petite woman and holding her hand. He let her in the passenger side of his blue Protégé, then walked around, and caught my eye as I glared at him. He lifted his arm to wave and then, with a look of confusion, thought better of it and got into his car and drove off.

"I have to get Ramona out of my head," I said out loud.

More waves came over me, waves of insatiable desire and fear. There was no neurotransmitter to nullify panic attacks. Being an adrenaline junkie didn't help.

I waffled from needing desperately to drive over to Ramona's condo, to having a red-hot lead ball of fear in my gut.

"I need to find out everything I can about her," I said as I put the Skyline into gear and steered onto the road.

What I needed was to find something, anything, to make me hate her. As I drove, I felt as though a gapping crevasse was ripping up the earth in front of me and that I was headed for a long, hard fall.

26

"Ramona Roos," I told Mahood when I called him early the next morning. "I need everything I can get on her." By ten a.m., he'd e-mailed me the scanty info they had.

Ramona Roos—

- Twenty-seven years old.
- Born March 5, 1984, to Larry and Monica Roos.
- Monica Roos, nee Knight, was Vincent Knight's sister. She committed suicide in 2001.
- Ramona Roos is the niece of Lone Wolf president Vincent Knight.
- Larry Roos sold construction equipment for Georgeson Industries. He currently lives in Victoria and is an alcoholic and lives on a disability pension.
- Ramona seems to have had a relatively normal upbringing. She attended Terry Fox High School in Port Coquitlam before studying computer science at BCIT.

- Roos was twice arrested for assault, once at age sixteen, after her mother's death, and again at age eighteen. No charges were laid.
- Ramona Roos may be an integral part of the Lone Wolves' computer fraud schemes, although CSIS computer forensic experts have been unable to definitively link her or the Lone Wolves to cyber-crime, such as infecting computers with viruses that detect keystrokes and render personal infor-mation and bank accounts vulnerable.
- In one case, a Sacramento man claims he made contact with Ramona Roos through her domina-tion Web site, and shortly thereafter his computer was taken over and his bank accounts ransacked. The money was not traceable. Many more victims of fraud and extortion are married and afraid to come forward.

There wasn't much in Mahood's report I didn't already suspect. It didn't surprise me that they had nothing on Ramona other than suspicion. The average person has no clue how exposed their computers are and how easy it is for criminals to rob them without them knowing, often from distant countries that have no resources or motive to chase down cybercriminals. The report also had addresses of known property and associates, which were incon-sequential to me at this stage.

It's a lot easier to pilfer someone's savings when you never see them, or in Ramona's case, when you're dealing with a bunch of whackos who fantasize being financially dominated by a woman they've never met. Scrolling through her Web site again, it was apparent from comments left by various men that some even agreed to consensual extortion and blackmail. They got some kind of thrill out of it. Most went back for more. Ramona's Internet competition was primarily unsophisticated dommes who probably hired webmasters for their sites and were not running the show on their own.

"The next time you're at her place, borrow her computer and e-mail me," Mahood told me. "I'll e-mail you back with a link. Open it. We'll get her computer."

"I doubt very much she'd let me use it," I said. "She probably has a few computers, for personal and business. The only other person I've seen in the room is Mia, and she's just there to…" I cut myself short.

It was a plan, though, one I'd try if I got the opportunity. I could even attempt to install a remote pinhole camera to watch her log on and get on it myself when she was sleeping.

The phone rang, startling me. I picked it up. It was Ramona. It was as if she had a seventh sense.

"What're you up to?" she said, her voice sounding tinny.

"Late night?" I asked.

"No later than usual. My life is one huge organizational nightmare," she said. "And I can't rely on anyone."

"Thanks," I replied.

"A heads up," she said, ignoring my dig. "O's got a hard-on, and he's looking all over for you. He came here in a huff. I got rid of him, straightened him out, for now. If he sees you first…"

"Not possible," I said. "O's fucked-up, but not nearly as badly as I am."

"You're making a lot of friends and a lot of enemies very quickly," Ramona noted. "Luckily I'm a friend, as long as I get what I want from you. Am I going to keep getting what I want?"

"I'm a rag you wring out," I said, saying what she wanted to hear, and just maybe a little of what I felt.

She laughed at that and said, "I'd like to go to the Cactus Club on Pemberton for a drink and dinner. Pick me up at seven. I'll make reservations."

"I'll see you then."

I hung up the phone with a nauseous feeling in my bones. The impression I got from the rank odor of this group of people was not unlike the smell of a rotting corpse. Rotting corpses all smell alike. It's the kind of overall sensation that's impossible to describe. Whereas a bloody scene has the taste much like sucking on a mouthful of coins, dead and bloated bodies have an overpowering, acidic sourness with the taste of feces dropped in like an olive into a martini. Marty, Marc, Vincent, the Ngs, O, Ramona, all gave off the stench of putrefaction, of impending doom, but for whom or what I couldn't say. They dressed well, drove expensive cars, and usually had large, beautiful homes, but like with the successful fishmonger, finery can't hide the stink.

I put on a rust-colored Caballero dress shirt that had a mandarin collar and blue jeans, shrugged into my brown

Caballero leather jacket, laced up a pair of Bostonian Tuscanas, and regarded myself in the hall mirror. Somewhere along the way I'd stopped smiling. I had a permanent, fixed jaw and eyes as black as shorl. There wasn't much I could do about it. There wasn't much I wanted to do about it. It's probably what Ramona liked about me. I stared at myself long and hard.

"Whatever happens," I said aloud, "make sure you can look yourself in the eye."

I stepped out into the hallway with the distinct feeling that I was descending into a deep, dank, arachnid-infested cave.

27

I got to Ramona's right at seven and pulled into the horseshoe drive of her building. The glass door swung open, and Ramona came out looking like a movie star sans the red carpet. She wore black boots that ended in a sharp angle at her knees, sheer stockings, and a ribbed black and white dress. Aside from a tattoo of a red, green, and blue butterfly visible on her left arm, she looked as sweet and innocent as a girl stepping out to her prom. My eyes were riveted to her muscular frame to which the dress clung like saran wrap.

She stepped into the Skyline and leaned over to kiss me like a normal couple might kiss. I was as normal as she'd ever get, which wasn't saying much for either of us. After returning from Afghanistan, I'd almost lost interest in any woman. I'd lost interest in anything but the need to dull the pain that barked in my ear all day long like a rabid junkyard dog. Ramona had changed that, which was no small feat.

Ramona smelled like cocoa butter and eucalyptus. Her nails were French manicured, and her strong, lovely hands created in me a longing to be squeezed by them mercilessly. Her dark hair had been highlighted and was wavier than I recalled. I slipped on a pair of brown leather driving gloves and remembered a day on patrol in the desert when our squad stepped through an opening in a wall, where IEDs were often buried, to find a dead, bloated body. There were no clothes on it, and it was impossible to tell whether it had been a man or woman. I took the wrists and Russell Gates took the ankles so that we could move the body aside. The skin of the hands slipped off like gloves. Disgusted, I tossed the skin aside, removed my own gloves and threw them at the corpse.

No one had laughed. No one had said anything. We'd managed to move the body a few feet, enough to clear the way. The stench was still there, in my nose, as well as the cloud of buzzing flies.

"What's the matter?" Ramona said.

"Hm? Oh, nothing." I shook my head and snapped the gloves tightly around my fists, put the shifter into first, and headed south on Lonsdale with the plan of heading west on 13th.

In the rearview mirror, I could see a '69 Camaro pull from the curb and follow us. It was black and polished to a high gloss, with wide slicks on the back and narrow pizza cutters on the front. This was a point A to point B racer, so the fuck wouldn't be able to stay with me if I gave the Skyline a workout. This 785 hp, all-wheel drive Japanese racer might have been the fastest street-legal car on the lower mainland.

I purposefully slowed to see what the Camaro driver would do. He slowed too.

"Got your seatbelt on?" I asked.

"Yeah," Ramona replied.

"Hang on."

In second gear, I smoked all four tires and drifted left onto Sixteenth. I could hear the loud braaap sound of the Chevy big block accelerate. I circled the block and came around again to Lonsdale and booted it south, looking for the Camaro. It was gone. Now a silver Viper with orange racing stripes up the hood was on my tail.

"What the fuck," I said. I reduced my speed to forty and let him follow me about five car lengths back. It was impossible to see through the glare of their windscreen to who was inside.

"Who is it?" Ramona asked.

"I was hoping you'd know," I said. "O probably. Get ready to duck."

At 13th the light turned yellow, and I gunned it. The Skyline hit 100km/h in 3.8 seconds. I made it through the intersection and left the Viper at the light. Rather than running, I pulled over two blocks down, got out, and opened the trunk and found the M10 and hid it under my Caballero.

"Wait here," I told Ramona.

I stepped quickly to a cube van parked two stalls behind me and emerged from behind it as the Viper neared. It was still daylight, but traffic wasn't heavy. The Viper didn't see me yet. I could see the business end of a sawed-off peeking at an odd angle over the passenger's right arm. I opened my jacket, flashing the M10 while screening it with the jacket flap. The fucker almost didn't see me at first. It was

O riding shotgun. He saw me late. His shoulder was stiff, from the corkscrew I suspected. His gaze fixed onto the M10, and that was when I closed the flap. He pointed to the distance, and the driver squealed the tires and flew down Lonsdale toward the quay.

I glanced around me to make sure no one besides O had seen the M10, shuffled back to the Skyline, and put the gun away and stepped in.

"It was O," I told Ramona.

"Take it easy," she said, her hand on my arm. "You're going to break the steering wheel."

"It's just an adrenaline dump," I told her.

As fucked in the head as the Lone Wolves were, they at least didn't make business a personal thing, unless that was good for business. This was what separated them from the peons who did their mule work. Ng, O, and their ilk were young, sociopathic know-it-alls with piss-poor egos that couldn't handle an insult or a broken nose without taking revenge. I'd have to take them out, or I'd be chased down and shot. Time to *X* O.

Dinner was fine, especially since Ramona paid.

"Courtesy of one of my Calgary slaves," she said.

I had salmon and a Guinness; Ramona had a lingcod burger with yam fries and a crantini, but not before her speech on the ills of red meat eating. I tried to look patient. I got through it concentrating on her perfectly molded breasts. She looked better than any of the servers, which is saying something at the Cactus Club.

"Still rattled?" Ramona asked.

"No," I said. "Just fantasizing about those thighs wrapping my face like an anaconda."

Ramona didn't like anyone else making suggestions. If it wasn't her idea, it wasn't going to happen.

"How come you don't have questions about me?" she asked sullenly.

"I know everything I need to," I said, which I thought was funny. "Seriously? I'm not into the revealing interview/date, where you reel off the same shit to everyone you see. Anyway, I don't see this as a date."

"What is it then?"

"I don't know. Two friends having dinner? You don't strike me as someone who wants a relationship. You're... not like that."

This comment frustrated her, but she discarded it quickly with a roll of her eyes. On our way out, Ramona's boots clacked across the stone path, her gait feminine and distinct. I would be able to discern till the day I died the sound of Ramona's footfalls. She took my hand and held it as we walked to the car.

28

Ramona hadn't seen my face for an hour when she finally tired and fell asleep. I crept out of bed to the kitchen, got a glass of grapefruit juice from the fridge, and then went to her office after double-checking to make sure she was asleep. I woke the computer, but I needed her password to get in. I went to the front hall and got the pinhole camera out of my Caballero but couldn't find an adequate spot to affix the damn thing. In my rooting, I came across a small photo album and opened it.

Inside were only about forty pages framing single photos dating from before the digital age. The little girl at the beginning could have been Ramona; the ones in the middle and near the end definitely were. In the pictures, she was doing childhood things: riding a tricycle, playing in the backyard with friends, dancing on stage, making snow angels, opening Christmas presents, sitting at a table at a holiday, the turkey looking bigger than she. Everything in the pictures looked so normal and was such a contrast to the woman who lay sleeping in the next room I dropped the album onto the desktop like it was a dead mouse, took a deep breath, and returned to bed.

Ramona lay facing the window, breathing quietly, murmuring softly under the duvet. A rectangle of slatted street light fell on her form, rising and falling with her breath. I lay wide-eyed for two hours, jacked and unable to sleep. I was used to my own bed. That was where I had coped the last two years.

In her sleep, Ramona snuggled close to my body, causing me to overheat. I slid away from her. None of us is smooth, I thought; we all have edges and angles. No one is pure, evil or otherwise, Limbaugh, Cheney, and Rove aside. I've heard of people having normal conversations with Bill O'Reilly, though I doubted it myself.

How had that girl gotten to this? Hell, I was lying beside her and had just buried my tongue as deep inside her as was possible. How the fuck had I gotten to this?

I didn't remember falling asleep. When I woke, the clock radio said 10:09. I could hear the shower and Ramona singing in a melancholic tone, like rain would sound if it could play a piano.

I fired up the ole transmitter out of habit and headed to the kitchen in my underwear and started the coffee maker. I decided to ask Ramona if I could e-mail from her office computer.

"Ramona?" I said through the steam in the bathroom. She liked it hot.

"Yo."

"Can I check my e-mail on your computer?"

"Sure."

I paused before asking, "Do I need a password to get on?"

"Oh, yeah. *Deathsentence*, one word."

"Deathsentence?"

"Deathsentence."

How appropriate, I thought. I closed the door and turned on the fan.

"Leave the fan off," Ramona yelled.

I flipped off the switch.

I phoned Mahood on my cell and told him I was getting on Ramona's computer, and then e-mailed him and waited for his response. When it came, I opened the link, giving CSIS access to Ramona's innermost secrets. Hey, it's what she did to her marks.

"Hey, sweetheart," she said to me when it was my turn to shower. In an angled closet-door mirror I could see her regard me, her face wrinkled with unanswered questions. She held my shoulder while she stood on her toes and kissed me. "What's wrong?"

"Nothing," I said.

Even though later in the day it would be time for her to bilk losers out of their money, I couldn't help guilt weighing me down like a ten-pound spinner hat.

"How do you want your eggs?" Ramona said when I had put on the same clothes I'd worn the night before and made my way to the island's marble counter.

"Over sleazy."

She wore a purple satin dressing gown and fuzzy purple slippers. Her hair was still damp when I stood next to her and kissed her on the temple. Already she seemed distant, like now wasn't the time. She was like a strobe light, flickering on and off to her own beat. I could feel the iciness. Maybe that was why she kept the shower so hot—to melt her innards. All of it gave me a raging headache.

When I left Ramona in her office, it was not yet noon. It was a crisp, sunny day that smelled like cherry blossoms, the sky whitened by a bleached sun. On my way to my car, a cruiser passed by, the driver slowing and peering at me with interest. He didn't stop.

An old woman walked slowly past me as I stood next to the Skyline pulling on my driving gloves. She saw me and said, "Hi," but her voice cracked, and I sensed fear in the way her limbs moved jerkily while she went away from me.

I stood back and looked at myself in the glass. Like a man with bad breath, I gave off a stink and didn't know it. It'd do me good to find out what it was, and soon.

29

I sat at my kitchen table with a cup of mud in my shaky mitt and read the headline:

Two Men Murdered

Vancouver: Two members of the Red-Legged Tarantulas were found dead in a home near UBC yesterday. Integrated Homicide Investigative Team spokeswoman Lise Cruz told reporters that it appeared to be a gangland hit and that several members of the MP gang were being questioned.

Three hydro workers found the bodies. One of the men, who wished to remain anonymous, said one victim had been beaten literally to a pulp, the second found with a corkscrew twisted into his forehead.

"We've asked witnesses to keep quiet from this point forward," Cruz said. "It is important for our investigators that these kinds of details not be released to the public."

The large home in the otherwise quiet street was cordoned off as crime scene investigators studied the scene.

One of the victims was Charles O. The second victim has not yet been identified.

Not a clue. The other man was Danny Ng. I wondered what Lyle was thinking right about now.

After that, Ramona and the Lone Wolves treated me differently. They didn't know, but they did know. The way they dealt with me was the same way a terrorist bomb builder would regard wires that needed to be twisted together.

"I have work for you," Marty said to me when he called later that morning. "Come over this afternoon and I'll apprise you."

"Apprise me?"

I found myself stepping more cautiously as I headed for the parking garage. Outside the sky was a sheet of even gunmetal grey. Traffic was slow on the Trans-Canada. I exited at 96th, and as I passed farm houses and fields, I turned on the Sirius. Acoustic guitar and Jay Malinowski's voice piped from the Bose speakers:

> What's done is done
> Life is a gun
> Life is a gun
> On the run

Marty was outside when I reached his acreage, spinning a wrench around a bone-dry spigot at the side of his home. He wore oily jeans and a blue denim shirt. His property looked better in the dim light, like a stripper looks better away from the fluorescents. I stepped from my car. Marty rose from his stooped position and arched his stiff back, avoiding looking at me. He smiled when I neared him, but really just bared his teeth in what looked like a death mask.

"Hear about O?" Marty asked. He looked at me with his head cocked at an odd angle.

"Read it in this morning's paper. He followed Ramona and me the other night, with a sawed-off."

"This your way of getting even?"

The muscles on Marty's face were stiff, as if rigor mortis had set in. I'd thought about this eventuality and had decided neither to admit nor deny involvement. Denying it made me a liar, but admitting it made me more vulnerable.

"Hey, whatever happened, he had it coming."

Marty laughed too loud, dropped the wrench he'd been holding at his side, and asked me if I wanted a beer.

"Sure."

We stood on the deck leaning against the railing. Marty was like most bikers in that he was always pushing a beer or drink into your hand, but unique in his penchant for good beer. His fridge was stocked with fifteen varieties.

This Hobgoblin beer, made by Wychwood, had a hint of fruit and quite the kick. I sipped slowly.

"We have a drop in Tofino that'll be heading out on a Citation later this week," Marty said. "I need you there to facilitate the transactions. Rent a camper van and go with Ramona. Spend a couple of days there."

"Tofino airport's a drop zone?"

Marty looked at me over the neck of his beer bottle and said, "We need fucking traffic controllers there, no pun intended. Sometimes it comes in by boat, goes out on plane. Sometimes the other way around. Sometimes it leaves on a truck. The fucking town's asleep. There's like four cops there even in tourist season."

"Who are we dealing with?"

Marty looked at me with torpor filling his eye sockets.

I looked straight out over the field toward a cottony clump of trees on the next property.

Marty guzzled from his bottle and said, "Tom Harvey is there now. Associates flying from Calgary are picking it up. Vincent wants you there representing."

"So BC bud goes out—cocaine, heroin, and ecstasy come back. Who do you trade with mostly?"

"Everyone and anyone. Mexico right now is a gong show, though. They're not cooperating with each other down there. The number of hits is off the dial. It's a chance for new suppliers to get into the market."

Marty coughed and fired a sluicing stream of brown spit onto the lawn below. I turned and leaned on the deck, facing the house. It was a house, but dead like the man who owned it.

"The heroin comes from South America?" I asked, knowing better.

He shook his head. "We have a Chinese supplier now in Southeast Asia who routes his shit through North Korea, if you can believe it. Myanmar, Cambodia, Laos are all hotspots."

"Oh, Chang Liu?" I said, citing a name I'd heard in the news, knowing if it was him the CSIS wouldn't need me.

"I only know him as Mr. Xy. He smuggles everything from DVDs into Brazil to Gucci bags into New York. His network is so fucking huge, he doesn't even care about shipments getting found from time to time. It's like us with grow ops, I guess," Marty said, shrugging. "We don't give a shit if we lose a house here and there. What's a $600,000 house when you're raking in millions?"

I mulled that over.

"I wouldn't be telling you this shit, except you've been through the fire for us," Marty said. "Normally I'd put a bullet between your eyes for asking."

"I'm a major jobber," I told him. "I won't do it without knowing what the fuck."

I'd probed enough for now and decided to change the subject.

Marty had been raising the beer bottle to his mouth to drink when I said, "A couple of nights in a camper van with Ramona? Don't know if I can handle it." He turned his head to look at me but kept pouring, the beer running down the front of his shirt.

30

I rented a white Dodge camper van trimmed in teal and waited two solid hours for Ramona to pack.

"It's just Tofino. We'll only be gone two days," I said.

When Ramona came out of her bedroom, she had on a Surf Sister top, Capri jeans, and a pair of cork-soled sandals. She had a duffel bag in her hand and ignored me when she walked past.

"Let me call Mia," she said.

Ramona picked up her iPhone and went into her office and shut the door. I could only hear the odd word or phrase.

"Make sure you're here..." And, "Put the money beside..." Ramona came out of the office and said sternly into the phone, "And no more complaining. I'm tired of it. There are plenty more where you came from."

I pretended I hadn't been listening when she stood in front of me, as if to say, "Well, I'm ready to go, are you?"

Of course, she complained about the van.

"I had a hard time finding one with 2,300 square feet and a walk-in closet," I said.

"Why couldn't we stay in a room? I have fake ID."

"And everywhere you go these days, they have security cameras. I have reservations at Crystal Cove. It's shoulder season. It'll be fine."

Ramona sulked all the way to Horseshoe Bay. On the ferry, she strolled around and around, soaking in looks from gawkers. I avoided her mood by gluing myself to the magazine rack in the store.

Once we hit Nanaimo, Ramona's mood switched for the better. The further we got from Vancouver, the more her spirits lifted. When we came to Cathedral Grove and the massive, towering tree trunks, I asked if she wanted to stop.

"Why? They're fucking trees for Christ's sake."

"That's one way of looking at it."

Ramona leaned back, kicked off her shoes and put her feet on the dash, wriggled her toes, and said, "Be careful with these. They make me a lot of money."

By the time we reached Port Alberni, I couldn't take it anymore. I pulled into the Wal-Mart lot far away from any other vehicle, drew the curtains, and fucked her on the fold-down bed. In the middle of it all she managed to say, "This is what Mia does for me. All day."

There was nothing in that comment for me, so I let it drift out the air vent.

Afterward we lay together listening to the stereo while some idiot managed to park beside us even though I was twenty meters away from the next car. We took time for lunch, and when we headed for Tofino, Ramona sat behind the wheel. I tried sleeping in the back.

"Have you met this Harvey dude?" she asked. She had a wad of Double-Bubble in her mouth and cracked it between her molars.

"No. It doesn't matter. I'm just there to facilitate."

Ramona laughed out loud. It was the first time I'd heard her laugh like that. It was the way a child might laugh if she was afraid of a backhand from an alcoholic father. I thought of the photo album.

"Facilitate? That's what you do? Facilitate? Ah, Char, the Great Facilitator."

When we reached the junction Ramona stopped at the park visitors' center and used the washroom. I stood and stretched and watched a white woman step out of the longest motor home I'd ever seen and waddle over toward the steps. There were California plates on her vehicle and a McCain/Palin sticker slapped crookedly on the bumper. The woman must have weighed six hundred pounds if she weighed an ounce.

Ramona passed the American as she came down the steps, sidled up to me, and said, "Well, now that we've been whale watching, I guess we can go home. Oh, look, Char can smile. How about that?"

Ramona leaned up and kissed me and, with her index finger, wiped lipstick from my mouth and tossed me the keys.

We passed Long Beach and stopped long enough to see a sheet of water so flat and glassy I thought we were looking out over the Dead Sea. A legion of frustrated surfers stood on the beachhead complaining about it.

"Guess that's why they call it Pacific," Ramona said to one of them.

The airport was just up the bluff. I took a drive onto Long Beach Golf Course property, passed the mini golf, and stopped when I came to the apron. There were two Cessnas parked there and a large jet helicopter. I turned around and headed back to the highway and Crystal Cove. When we'd found our manicured site, we drove to The Point Restaurant at the Wickinninish Inn. After that, we headed to Tonquin Road to meet with Harvey at his home overlooking the ocean and Vargas Island.

The house was two levels and painted light blue. Moss or mold grew along the length of the boards. A large, untreated grey cedar deck surrounded the entire affair. In the middle of the home was a massive, stone fireplace from which smoke drifted lazily in thin whorls. I could smell cedar and alder.

"This is the address," Ramona said, looking in her purse and finding a slip of paper with Marty's handwriting on it. I parked behind a massive black on black Suburban. The temperature had dropped, and I put on a thermal jacket and turned up the collars. Ramona slipped on a white down vest and took my hand.

We stepped carefully along uneven pavers. No lights were on in the house, but I sensed a presence on the deck around front. We walked up the back stairs, and from there we could see the beach below and a fire burning and about thirty stinking hippies drinking beer and wine. Bongo beats drifted up.

"Where's your gun?" Ramona said disparagingly.

Ramona and I turned the corner and stopped dead. Standing on the deck and facing us, a thin, broad smile spread across his face like a gash, was the biggest fucking Indian I'd ever seen. He stood 6'9" or more and looked a lot like a cedar stump with arms and legs. He had on a homemade sleeveless shirt with "I'm very excited to be here" written across the front in green felt. His head was the size, shape, and color of an NBA basketball, but with less hair and no logo.

He laughed, a laugh that sounded like a bicycle chain grinding against the sprocket. Ramona squeezed my hand. I squeezed back.

"Harvey. Tom Harvey," the eclipse said, extending his relatively small hand for us to shake. "My friends call me Mini-me."

The thought that ran through my head was: *What the fuck do they need me for?*

31

Sensing how uncomfortable he made some people feel, Mini-me acted apologetic about his height and size and leaned against the deck railing to compensate. I eyed the nails to see if they'd hold. At one point, he went inside and came out with a wrist rocket and fired a pebble high into the air between two Sitka trees. The stone came straight down on the revelers on the beach below. We looked away, but there was no way they could've seen who'd fired the rock. The group eventually made its way to the far cove, away from any houses.

"They're flying in tomorrow," Mini-me said, "at two. They'll get here around two thirty, three o'clock."

He didn't invite us inside or offer us a beer. His barbeque was on, but the lid was closed. The sizzle said steak.

"What're they driving?"

Mini-me shook his huge, orange head and said, "Not sure. They're renting from Budget. Park in the visitors' parking, across the street. Be here before two. Gimmee your cell number in case."

The sun was setting, but a wide band of clouds on the horizon erased the hope of a beautiful sunset. Mini-me's tone sounded like "good-bye" to me, so Ramona and I left the gargantuan Indian and decided to head back to the campsite.

The fresh air was putting Ramona to sleep. She took off to the common shower, and when she returned, she made up the bed and dove under the covers. Under the pretext of taking my own shower, I grabbed my towel and left Ramona in the camper. I stepped behind the shower building and dialed Mahood on my cell phone.

"Yeah." It was Mahood, and he knew it was me on the line.

"Two o'clock tomorrow a Citation is landing at the Tofino airport, bringing cash and goods, receiving goods and flying right out. They're renting a car from Budget to drive to a house on Tonquin." I gave Mahood the address and filled him in.

"Good work," Mahood said, his voice mournful, plaintive.

I didn't ask. I wasn't his friend, didn't want to be. I was beginning to think that in their own fashion law enforcement were as fucked up as the people they were trying to catch.

I showered because that's where I had supposedly gone. When I got back to the campsite, a small commotion at a cabin behind the camper was just ending. A man with a Russian accent was losing an argument with a three-hundred-pound security guard. There was a party in the hot tub, and the whole shebang shut down when the guard went to a control panel and shut off power to the cabin.

"Nothing like flipping switches," I said to myself.

This night I slept well: apparently it was Ramona who tossed and turned. Luckily for me, the bed was made of memory foam and didn't jiggle each time she rolled over.

In the morning I lay still, listening to the wind whoosh through the treetops and Ramona complain about her lack of sleep, thinking, it's one big, fucking board game, with rules set by the owners, the odds stacked against the average Joe. In my mind, I was seeing my work, Mahood's work, getting nowhere in the end. Cleaning up crime is like pulling up Scottish broom: you need to get all of it by the roots to rid it from the landscape. It was never going to happen. All you could do is clear your yard of it, help your neighbor do the same, and then go watch a fucking hockey game or CSI, where everything gets solved by good-looking people in an hour. Right.

Ramona spent the whole morning on the phone, so I went to the beach and watched a coastguard vessel practice off the coast. On the horizon, the silhouette of a carrier ship drifted eastward.

I went back to the camper van, but Ramona wasn't there. I found her at the main office complaining to a seventeen-year-old clerk about some useless annoyance. I grabbed her by the arm and led her out to the van and took her for a continental breakfast at the Long Beach Lodge while we sat by the fire and stared out at a sheet of grey-blue glass that stretched from there to Japan.

We'd finished our breakfast and had our coffees refilled when my phone rang.

"They're here early," Mini-me said, sounding panicked. "Can you get over here now?"

"I can be there in ten."

I hung up and said to Ramona, "I don't like this. Mini-me's scared shitless."

"He's a huge guy—doesn't mean he's tough."

We left our coffee cups half full and drove sanely to Tonquin Road and parked across from Mini-me's house. I went into the back of the van, flipped up the seat, and reached for the M10 in the compartment beneath and shoved it and the Sig Mosquito into a holster and put on my Caballero over it and stood outside and checked myself in the mirrored side window on the van.

Ramona hadn't brought a gun, so I gave her a snub-nosed .38 that had a soft rubber grip, which she put in her purse without pause, as if I'd handed her a pencil. Her manicured fingers looked lovely wrapped around the weapon.

"The safety…" I said, but got cut off.

"I know. Don't worry about it. I've been to the range a thousand times," she said, using her fingers to put quotation marks around the word *range*.

We walked calmly to the house. Mini-me was at the back landing. He wore a Hornets warm-up suit that had to be quadruple-*x*. This time he let us in.

The home had been built in the 70s and hadn't been updated since. The tiled counters and floors were done in earthy dark greens and shades of grey brown. He took us through the kitchen to the living room. The large picture window looked out over lava rock and ocean. A large sectional was caved and warped on one side, where Mini-me probably hauled out. The coffee and end tables were mismatched. A large, bright, beautiful Hobson painting of a sea lion in a kelp forest hung on the main wall, making the rest of the dump look even more dull and boring. The entire house smelled like a cedar that had Doritos for leaves.

"Have you met the men coming?" I asked Mini-me.

Mini-me shook his head no but said, "Once."

Ramona looked at me quizzically when she noticed the sweat beading on Mini-me's forehead.

"Maybe you stand over there when they come," Mini-me said, "blocking the entrance to the kitchen. Better if you're standing. She can sit on the couch, over there by the sliding doors."

"Why so nervous, big man?" I asked.

He shook his head as if to negate the question and said, "The last time...a little nerve-racking. I get paid to cross shipments. I'm not a big-league player. Guns make my ass nervous. Whitey makes my ass nervous"

Ramona took her seat on the couch, her purse close at hand. Mini-me stood with his hands in his pant pockets. I leaned against the door frame. On the mantle, a clock ticked, slowly, reminding me of the time bomb that was always nascent in my thoughts.

I stood with Mini-me in the gloom, listening to Ramona crack her gum and watching her cross her legs and nervously rock her foot up and down. Ten minutes passed, and then we could hear the whir of an engine pull into the drive. I turned around and stepped to the kitchen window to see.

Three average-sized men dressed in jeans and collared shirts got out and went to the rear door of their silver SUV. They were behind salal and devil's club, and I couldn't see them well from there.

Mini-me took off down the hallway to one of the bedrooms, moving faster than any man that size has a right to.

"Your uncle wouldn't put you in harm's way, would he?" I asked Ramona. I smiled broadly.

"You are the biggest idiot on the face of the earth."

Mini-me came out of the bedroom hoisting three large fish totes and set them down on the living room floor.

"Game on," he said, breathing heavily. His knife wound smile spread across his rotund head. He clapped his hands together and rose up on the balls of his feet. Maybe he didn't like guns, but sure did like the rush he was getting now.

32

One of the traders stepped from behind the SUV. He was about 5'9" and no more than 135 pounds, with thick, brown hair and deep-set asymmetrical eyes that were too close together. The second man was taller, thinner, with curly reddish hair and freckled skin. He stood straight and inflated his chest when he saw me. Both these men were in their late thirties or early forties. Whitey the boss man was some piece of work.

Whitey was blond-haired and green-eyed and had an oddly attractive, Mongolian shape to his otherwise Caucasian face. His eyes were narrow slits and his cheekbones high and puffed.

As they came up to the deck carrying two medium-sized cardboard boxes each, Whitey spoke to the others in a language I couldn't place, and I'd been around. But by the time they had climbed the stairs and were on the back deck, Whitey was at the front and speaking for them in perfect upper-class English.

"Nice to see you again, Mr. Harvey," he said, but he was looking at me. His eyes were electric in their shade and luminescence, like bicycle reflectors. The general effect of his gaze was hypnotic.

"The shit's inside, in the living room," Mini-me said. "I packed it in fish totes, like you wanted."

Whatever Mini-me felt, he appeared confident and assured. I had an inkling his lummox act was exactly that: an act.

The three men stood on the deck at the top of the stairs and signaled for us to enter. We filed inside and made our way to the living room. Ramona sat watching us, her purse near her right hand, not looking conspicuous.

"Who are these people, Tom?" Whitey asked. "I'm not bloody comfortable with people I don't know."

Whitey's teeth were many and jutted out at odd angles, like a piranha's. It was a contrast to his strangely attractive features.

"It doesn't matter who the fuck I am," I said. "I'm here. Do this thing and be on your way."

Whitey stood in the middle of the living room with the other two a step behind, one on either side, looking at me like I was the dummy. I took up my position in the doorway. Mini-me stood with his hands in his pockets in front of Whitey, a coffee table on which the cardboard boxes now rested between them. Mini-me sensed Whitey's discomfort with that pose and brought his hands out to his sides.

Mini-me opened three of the cardboard boxes packed with heroin and ecstasy tablets. Whitey opened the fish totes and inspected the bud. Mini-me then opened the three boxes containing cash and didn't count it but ascertained that there was no filler before closing up the boxes.

I reached into my jacket for a pack of gum, took a piece for myself, and threw one to Ramona. I held the pack, waiting to see if anyone made a move.

In perfect synchronicity, Whitey's henchmen reached behind their backs. As they did so, I feigned replacing the pack of gum and withdrew the silenced M10 like it was a newspaper I was reading and held it up in view but pointed toward the fireplace, just to impede any funny business. The Glocks mewled in the M10's presence, and the light went out of Whitey's bright green eyes.

Men like Vincent Knight get where they are not only because of the degree of psychopathy from which they suffer, but also from a sixth sense. They don't always win, but neither does Tiger.

"Now you know who I am, Whitey," I said.

Mini-me's paw halted me. Whitey seethed. The skin stretched taut over his face and twitched as if there were fire ants crawling on it.

If this insano's a grunt, who the fuck runs their show? I wondered.

I held up the M10 and pointed it at Whitey.

"Drop the Glocks, pick up the totes, and get the fuck out," I said. "I see guns the next time, you're hamburger, hear?"

The guns tumbled to the floor, and the three each took a tote and started toward the back door. I stepped into the hallway, watching them walk past.

"We have people at the airport, Whitey…" I said.

"Don't call me that," he blurted angrily.

No better way to get your nickname to stick than hating it.

He had the tote in his arms and no gun.

"Get in the truck, go to the airport, and get out, Whitey. Any problems and you don't take off. Comprende? By the way, we appreciate the business. Please come again."

The other two made their way down to the driveway. Whitey gathered himself and went carefully down the steps, which were slick with moisture, his body stiff with ire, his head angled awkwardly so that he could see where he was going.

When the totes were in the back of the SUV and all three had gotten in, the vehicle sat for an uncomfortable amount of time. It was difficult to see through the kitchen window, between the bushes, and through the windscreen, but I thought I saw Whitey shake his finger at the man who sat in the front passenger seat, and then hammer fist the steering wheel.

"That was tense there for a minute," Ramona said, coming up behind Mini-me.

"That's the way it's been the last few times," the big Indian said. "Taking liberties and seeing how far they can go, who they can push around."

"I doubt they'd have done anything," I said, "unless they were planning to heist their boss man as well."

"Xy? No fucking way, man," Mini-me said. "Are you fucking crazy?"

"No, but Whitey looks like his microprocessor's fried."

Mini-me slapped his forehead at my comment and looked at me like I was a talking dog.

"Who the fuck is Xy?" I asked, remembering Marty had said the name.

"I need a drink, man," Mini-me said, heading for the fridge. "Want a drink?"

He took from the fridge a bottle of Forty Creek, twisted off the cap, and poured two fingers into three highball glasses, held his up, and said, "Cheers."

Ramona threw back hers in one toss. I took a mouthful.

"Xy!" Mini-me exclaimed, shaking his head and giggling like an eleven-year-old girl. "Good ole X-Y-Xy."

33

As often as not, it's the limo driver or bag man who has the dope on everyone. Not to mention he's usually a lot smarter than anyone suspects. He's the common denominator, and word gets around any organization. Let's face it, though, the Lone Wolves aren't la cosa nostra. Hell, even la cosa nostra ain't la cosa nostra anymore.

"Take a look at this," Mini-me said after refilling his glass of Forty Creek.

We followed him to an office that had a 32" flat screen on the wall connected to his desktop Dell. He sat in the lone creaking chair and typed into the keyboard while Ramona and I stood behind him. The screen lit up. He navigated to Google Earth, and soon we were looking down onto an azure sea and two desolate rocks. Mini-me zoomed in.

"This is so fucking cool," he said. "Watch this."

The satellite picture was from an angle, as they can be. The southerly rock was jagged conical lava and looked about four hundred feet high, not a lick of life visible from our vantage. The northerly rock was slightly higher and shaped like a misshapen *W*, with tints of green and yellow and pink along the crest. White water frothed at the base of the rocks in the still shot.

Mini-me zoomed in further. High above the *W* was a citrate palace with an expansive courtyard that had a turquoise pool. Meandering down were hundreds of steps carved into the lava, leading down to moorage in a semiprotected cove, semiprotected in summer, I imagined. But on the far side of the *W* was a helicopter pad for easy access.

"Rumor has it that Xy has tunnels and underground bomb-proof chambers, and even a submarine dock. Have you heard of this dude, man?"

I shook my head dumbly and said, "Marty mentioned the name."

"Xy is attempting to bring the Southeast Asian heroin trade to North America. As it stands, most of the heroin that makes it to the US comes from Mexico or Columbia. Xy has huge markets in China, but he wants to spread out, to bring his product to world markets. Timely, considering the wars in Mexico.

"Xy got his start with a license to sell electronic addons, then branched to making fakes of fakes. He has factories in North Korea making products that say 'Made in China' on the bottom. He has industrial-sized factories buried underground, literally, and eventually had to leave China because the Communist Party began cleaning up corruption in his part of the world. He runs everything from his 'Palace of Justice,' as he calls it."

"How do you know all this?" Ramona asked him.

"Hey, man, I've been in on Vincent's dealings for a while. And everything's on the Web. There are areas of the

Internet where only techies chat. Regular people like you don't even know about them."

Ramona's expertise made her scowl at that comment, but Mini-me's knowledge left her in the dust.

"Guys like Xy don't care about the plate of food in front of them. They only care about what the waiter is carrying over. More, more, more."

"He backs Whitey?" I asked.

Mini-me nodded, took a gulp of whiskey, and said, "This year is their first foray here, and they aren't happy about Ng's death in Vancouver. Apparently they were grooming him for their invasion. They don't care for Vincent. I'm telling you, if these dudes ever get a foothold here…forget about it."

"And Xy runs the whole shebang?" I asked.

"He controls a half-dozen or so fiefdoms. He has ultimate control, money funnels back, but he sees the need for local decision makers. Hey, Toyota's decided they need to do the same. Attempts to deal with Vincent have soured somewhat, hence his wandering eyes."

"So Vancouver's little gang war gets more interesting," I said.

Ramona said, "What's the fucker look like?"

"Good question," Mini-me answered. "I've tried finding images of him before. Nothing comes up."

"It amazes me that he runs everything from that rock in the ocean. Whereabouts is it?" Ramona asked Mini-me.

"In the Eastern Sea, off Korea. He has offices in Dubai, too."

"Don't they all?" I said.

"Let me try something else," Mini-me said. "I think Xy is a nom de plume. I'll see if I can find his real name and search that. Or search his brother and find him that way."

It made sense a guy like Xy would keep his image unknown, but how do you do that in this day and age? Hell, we were just looking down his chimney.

Mini-me navigated to Wikipedia. He found no aliases, but on a link to an associate in Xy's early electronics business was a high-resolution image of two unseemly Chinese men.

"That's him," Mini-me said, tapping the screen to the man on the right. "See the snakehead tattoo on his right hand. I heard he had that."

I couldn't see the tattoo or the man, till Mini-me clicked on and enlarged the picture.

Mini-me spun around and looked at me and down at my hands.

"Holy shit," Ramona said, nudging me with her elbow. "He looks just like you."

If it was Xy, and I had no doubt Mini-me had his shit straight, he did look like me, exactly. He wore a beautiful white suite with a silver and black tie. The man beside him wasn't quite as tall or as handsome, but could have been a relative. It was like looking at myself in an alternate universe.

"Betcha Whitey and his boys have never seen Xy. They would've said something," Mini-me noted.

"It's spooky," Ramona said, looking at the photo, me, then the photo, and me again.

"What's the snakehead mean?" I asked.

"Mmm, not sure," Mini-me replied. "Snakeheads export migrant workers. I know he does that and infects them with his minions. But I've read that the tattoo goes all the way up his arm."

"Do the Chinese export anything decent?" Ramona asked, her refilled whiskey untouched.

Mini-me laughed and said, "No. Everything's a knock-off. Even their crime comes on the cheap. But their economy is not building a great country. In fact, it's busting it up. China is a collection of very unique peoples. There are tens of thousands of riots yearly. The Party doesn't tolerate competition where violence and corruption are concerned."

"Who's the guy with Xy? Do you know?" I asked.

"Probably his brother. He didn't get out in time. He disappeared in the prisons. They were being hunted down for their chain of brothels, which trafficked women and children from as far away as Afghanistan and Kyrgyzstan and Turkey, I hear."

"You couldn't dream this up," I said.

"The planet's going to hell in a handcart," Mini-me said, shifting noisily in his seat and putting his computer to sleep. This coming from a bona fide drug wholesaler. "The degree of control these cocksuckers have is mind-bending. Even governments like ours and the States don't have the resources to handle it. It's like they're handing out parking tickets in Chinatown."

I stood quietly, staring at the now blank screen.

"What's the matter?" Ramona asked me.

Mini-me stood and pulled up his pants and straight-ened his jacket.

"Just thinking," I told her. "Just thinking."

34

The first thing I did when I returned to Vancouver, after sleeping for ten straight hours, was call Mahood so that I could meet with him and update him on Xy, which was likely the name they were looking for, but I hoped it didn't mean an end to my work. I doubted it would, because the money I was depositing from my criminal activity was more than paying my contracted salary. Once they got a name, they'd need someone to pursue it.

The world seemed different to me after my trip to Tofino and the day spent with Mini-me explaining the vagaries of the shadow world. I thought it funny that the name Xy was pronounced "zee." There are no coincidences, just things God doesn't want his hand in, like bad puns.

I met Mahood in the back of an ice cream parlor in Fort Langley. Fort Langley was to Vancouver what a calm thought is to my mind: an escape. We sat next to a window with no one around us, so I was able to talk easily about it. I handed him a printout of a report, which he folded and placed in his pocket.

It was a warm, sunny day. Mahood had on a colorful, short-sleeved Bugatchi shirt embossed with ferns, beige slacks, and Italian loafers. He had a strawberry sherbet, and I had a chocolate ice cream on a waffle cone. He looked at me like I was Houdini and had just made a terrific escape.

"I'm not sure if this is the name L'Ouiseau is looking for, but it's pretty bang-on," I said. "I'm making good penetration, all based on my tie to that fat fuck Smuker. Ssfucker. I'm willing to stick it out."

"We have no plan on pulling you yet," Mahood reassured. His face was slightly tan, making him appear a few years younger than he was.

"Here's something else," I said, handing him a printout of Xy's picture that Mini-me had printed for me.

"What's this, your grad photo?"

"That's what I thought," I said, chuckling. "No. That's Xy, believe it or not."

Mahood held up the photo to me and studied Xy and me, side by side.

"Christ almighty, that'll tingle the old spine."

Halfway through our cones, we went out and walked down Glover to the river and leaned against a railing and gazed over to the island and a brilliant white church that had probably been built in the 1800s. The deciduous trees looked like giant luminescent cotton bolls. Sunlight seemed to dance through the air that blew briskly through the leaves. A CN train whizzed past, but even that was relaxing.

"You seem suited to the work," Mahood told me flatly. "Takes guts and fits you like a glove."

My mind's eye went back again to the bloated body and the cadaver's skin, which had fallen off when I'd tried moving it.

"CSIS agents give me the heebie-jeebies," I said. "No offence."

"None taken. Anyone who's served in Afghanistan is bound to make assumptions."

"Assumptions? I was there. They take their lead from the CIA. The Bush-Cheney CIA. Not a good foundation to start with."

"You've never broken the law to get where you needed to go?"

"You misunderstand me, my friend. I lament the possibility of becoming one of you. I mean, I don't see myself as a CSIS agent."

"That's because you're not."

"True. But I am an operative. I am a contractor of the CSIS. I am an associate, just like I'm an associate of the Lone Wolves. They're red and blue circles that overlap," I said. "There's one fuck of a lot of bruising, my friend."

A stretch of silence separated us for a minute as though a curtain had dropped between us.

"Did you get photos of Whitey and the jet?" I asked to change the subject.

Mahood nodded. "Hopefully we'll be able to tie it to this Xy character. Your girlfriend, well, there's a whole other ball of wax."

I waited for him to go on.

"We're not sure yet exactly how this is working, but we think that aside from phishing she has programs that essentially record keystrokes on personal computers. There's a shit load of money to be made doing this. A Russian criminal hacker, or cracker, was arrested last year, after pilfering $95,000,000 out of personal bank accounts around the world. They used downloads from porn sites and unauthorized music and DVD downloads to infect computers. Typically they don't empty accounts: that's too difficult. But if you have a million account numbers and take ten dollars out of each one, few will even notice, and no police are going to hunt someone down for ten bucks."

"You *think* Ramona's doing this?"

Mahood nodded and said, "The way they're set up, the e-mails are not emanating from their computers—they're coming from hijacked ones, and we have yet to figure out who is sorting through the personal information they're stealing, or where. It could be anywhere in the world."

"If it makes money, Ramona's doing it," I offered.

"We've got similar spyware on her computer, but if she's doing it from another location…"

Mahood looked at his watch. Suddenly he looked drawn and tired.

"Look, I got to splitnofski."

"Me too. Marty's calling me two-three times a day now."

He stood facing me, his fists balled and on his hips.

"Did you have anything to do with O's death?" he asked when he had stood back from the railing and faced me.

That was a simple technique I'd once used to grill an unfaithful girlfriend in high school: change subjects real fast, and then watch the eyes.

I'd been as meticulous as was possible with that set of events. I'd worn gloves and a balaclava, and everything had been burned, including the stolen car. And I have little body hair. The corkscrew was an idiotic calling card, especially if O had mentioned anything about our first romp together downtown. I promised myself I'd never again do anything that stupid, but it had been compulsive, as though I wanted the slightest of trails leading to me.

"That's out of the blue," I said, not knowing for sure what his instincts told him about me. I looked him dead-on.

"Look, we know your record, Char. Most people would get squeamish watching an autopsy on Discovery channel. You, on the other hand..."

He let the sentence sway in the wind.

My car was here, at the park. Mahood's was over by the ice cream parlor.

"Keep up the pace, Char. And don't get too involved in that psycho bitch. She'll rip your lungs out, Jim."

He smiled, but there was malevolence in the corners of his mouth, the way they curled when he smirked. He turned and walked away before I could say anything, which was probably good for me.

I got to my car, leaned inside the open window, and reached for my driving gloves. I was going through gloves like a fat kid goes through a pack of Smarties. I needed to find them in bulk.

On Glover I drove past Mahood, who was still walking to his car, hands in pockets, shoulders stooped. I stepped on the gas and rocketed westward, Mahood's form shrinking to the size of a mite in the rearview mirror.

35

I had no idyllic notions about the people I was dealing with in CSIS or the Lone Wolves. As if from the middle of my cranium, Pink Floyd's "Mother" drifted from the sound system:

> Mother, should I trust the government?
> Mother, will they put me in the firing line?
> Is it just a waste of time?

But even if there were corrupt CSIS agents, even if the Canadian government made bad decisions and orders, even if some members performed criminal acts, they weren't a criminal gang. The Lone Wolves were. The first moments I'd spent with Marty, Vincent, Ramona, Ng, and O convinced me to strike first and strike hard. No pussyfooting.

Most hardworking, honest citizens know about crime but resist notions of its endemic nature. My first step into a country like Afghanistan told a story I wish could be untold. Lack of regulations on the one hand and overregulation on the other creates opportunities for übercriminals who are willing to take the risk to step in. But it is the North Americans and Western Europeans buying the knock-offs because they're cheaper, buying the drugs that are smuggled, and going on holidays to use brothels outfitted with trafficked women and children that are the root of the problem. This, I decided as I screamed the Skyline along Lougheed highway, was the flaw with the free market ideology: Right-wing thinkers believe fanatically that rational demand will result in rational supply, and if we get rid of impediments like government rules and laws, all will be well. Problem with that thought is humans aren't rational, and if left to their own, society deteriorates rapidly.

I opened the window to shake the thoughts. What use was it worrying about something that would never change? A commander of mine had once said, "Worry twice as hard, see if that helps."

Marty wanted to meet me at La Casa del Habano, a cigar lounge downtown where he kept a three hundred dollar bottle of Scotch to drink along with his cigar of the day.

I stopped off at home to take my medication and then headed out the door and drove downtown. The lounge was easy to find. Marty was already there, dressed in a long-sleeved collared Ocean Pacific shirt and designer jeans, and looked like he'd just had a shave and a haircut, giving an entirely different impression than when he lounged alone in his sweats at home. Jekyll and Hyde.

He met me at the door and led me to the humidor, where he chose a Cohiba. I hummed and hawed and settled on a Punch cigar.

"Fitting," he said.

Marty led me to the lounge where he had his bottle on a table between two firm leather chairs facing each other. He poured us three fingers of Dallas Dhu and lit our cigars. Ice cream, Scotch, and cigars: the diet of champions.

"Tom told us how helpful you were last weekend," Marty said. Even his voice sounded clearer, in spite of the cigar.

I puffed and sipped. The cigar tasted like it had been sodden in port and wrapped in leather. The Scotch had a smooth chocolate and honey aroma. They went together like women and wine.

"He's one smart dude, man. You don't expect it looking at him."

"He's the one who called for back up, said things were getting more awkward each time. Vincent surrounds himself with high achievers."

"And you," I said, joking.

An older, handsome man with obvious plastic surgery tightening his face came into the room with a full-figured, sexy Latina with dark hair that was too long for her age and face, which I guessed to be around forty-five. Marty dropped the volume of his voice, but the couple sat at the other end of the room, far enough away that they couldn't hear our conversation. Both had cigars and had with them a bottle of 1792, a top-shelf bourbon.

"Anyway, we're having problems with associates who are feuding amongst themselves," Marty said. "Lyle Ng is gunning for Manny Rio. Heard of him?"

I shook my head no, but I was lying.

"Manny runs the MP gang: The Melting Pot. They're a ragtag collection of mutts, hence Melting Pot. Mutt Pot," he said, not laughing at his own attempt at a joke. "Anyway, they've been at each other's throats for nine months now. There were some hits at the River Rock. You may have read about it in the papers."

I nodded.

"Normally we don't care what these fuckers do, as long as it doesn't involve us. Problem is, we have good distribution with the Tarantulas and the MPs. It'd be a shame to start over with someone else, especially with our Chinese friend loitering offshore. And the more get killed off, the more losers try horning in."

Marty took a long tug on his Scotch and then puffed on the cigar and let out a cloud of smoke, which left the room swiftly through the air exchanger.

"I need you to accompany me to a little…meeting. That's a good word. We'll try to iron things out. If we can't, well, then there's another job for you. In the meantime, I need you to head up to Merritt. We have an associate there with a helicopter logging business becoming unreliable. I want you to handle it alone."

"You have a lot of 'associates,'" I said. "You want him, money, what?"

"He's getting too big for his britches. He's been complaining about the arrangement for a while, whining about his risks. Hell, if it wasn't for us, he'd have lost the business two years ago. Think these guys are making any money in logging now? Whatever you do, don't whack him. We need him."

Marty laughed at that like he thought I was his friend. Real friends eluded these fuckers.

"Manny Rio, eh?" I said. "I hear he's a good banger."

"Hey, he can't stop a bullet. I've seen him scrap though. He has trouble with big guys like me, but he's very, very fast. I'd like to see you and him swinging. Want another shot?" Marty asked.

"Naw, I like my driver's license."

Marty poured himself a snort, polished it off, and stubbed out his cigar.

"Just what the doctor ordered," he said as we stood.

Marty walked beside me as we left the club, his arm around me. "Say, you're a smart guy, tough, knows his way around. You wouldn't be thinking of screwing us, fucking us over, would you?" he said, grinning.

His arm was like a vice around my shoulder. I knew he doubted his chances against me, one on one, but the feeling was mutual. He was showing me either that he wasn't afraid of me or that I had more than just him to fear.

"Well, Marty," I said, putting my arm around him and laughing, laughing because he'd sounded so much like Mahood. "I do what I need to do, when I need to do it. When you've got a problem with that, you just let me know."

Outside we let go of one another. Trying to nail down these sociopaths is like log rolling. They're like a conundrum inside an enigma wrapped in a drunken, psychotic fury. But really their minds are simple. They follow a creed that emanates from a childhood of physical and sexual abuse, and they wear normalcy the way the Elephant Man might wear makeup to hide his face.

36

Sean Greer had his twenty-acre spread ten kilometers outside of Merritt, off the Coquihalla highway. I took the Skyline rather than the Tundra Marty offered. I wanted my presence to say "city."

The sky was clear and the road dry, but it was easy to see the treachery that lay in the ascending road with the slightest touch of weather. Bachman's Sledgehammer came through the Sirius satellite, reminding me of Ramona, whom I had a date with this evening after my trip to see Chopper-boy.

Marty had given me a newspaper clipping with a black-and-white photo. Greer was in his mid thirties and had a soft, round face that failed to intimidate even with the Van Dyke. He looked like the guy who installs your cable. The brief article that accompanied the photo told a tale of RCMP surveillance and failed attempts by law enforcement to nail down Greer's aircraft-smuggling operation.

Marty told me that shipments met helicopters at various prearranged points throughout southern B.C., and from there, the choppers would interrupt regular contract work with a jig south of the Forty-ninth. Reading the article at a coffee shop in Hope, I couldn't help but wonder how Greer couldn't be caught. It came down to vast expanses of wilderness and lack of manpower.

It was one o'clock when I reached the rural route to Greer's property. I hadn't made it a hundred yards down the gravel road, regretting taking the Skyline as pebbles bounced along the undercarriage, when his red Chevy pickup passed me and headed into Merritt. I stopped on the shoulder and pondered following him or heading to his property. I decided to head to his property.

Greer's business lay in a gulley and was protected by several lines of trees and lush vegetation that created a double-*x* pattern visible from above. I could see nothing else from the road. I found the access and drove along the S-shaped drive till I came upon a two-story split level home with long slabs of irregular siding painted brown and faded, with cheap thermal windows that were fogged in places even on this dry day, and two, large bare cinder block outbuildings.

I stopped the car in the empty lot in front of the house and studied the layout. A curtain moved and for a brief moment I saw a blonde holding a baby. She slipped through a doorway into a back room, the kitchen probably. She emerged from the back, and through the glare on the living room window, I could see she was on a cordless, calling Sean, no doubt. Suddenly my decision to come straight here when I'd seen Greer head into town seemed like a bad one. Now Sean had warning.

I got out of the car and headed toward the house. To my left, behind one of the outbuildings, I could see rotor blades strapped down against any wind. A few toys lay scattered, muddied, and battered by weather.

The front door opened, and a blonde with a medium build and holding her baby came out onto the six foot square landing and said, "We have children here. Sean's on his way back. I suggest you leave."

I wasn't wearing a jacket and had my weapons in the car. I held up my hands defensively and said, "I'm just here to talk business."

She wasn't buying it. She spun on her heels, her ponytail swaying back and forth when the front door slammed closed.

People on edge like this usually have good reason. I went to the car, shrugged on my Caballero, and went to the trunk, slipped the M10 into its holster, and buttoned it in, and not too soon. Three trucks piled with rednecks flew down the drive and grinded to a stop level with the Skyline, maybe thirty feet distant. I hadn't planned on doing anything but talk, hadn't planned on the M10 being anything but a confidence builder in case I needed one. But these were rednecks, in a part of the country where they have gun racks on their baby carriages.

A shotgun-toting dunce with a shaved and misshapen head came out of Greer's red truck. When I saw the gun, I pulled the M10. Nothing intimidates like an M10 that has a suppressor screwed into the barrel. If you don't know what it is, you guess it just by its impression, like the difference between a dentist's and executioner's chair. I pointed it directly at them over the roof of the Skyline after I'd backpedalled behind it.

The redneck with the shotgun looked confused. He pointed his weapon toward a clump of trees. His head looked like a stone you might see in a creek bed and think, Hey, that rock kinda looks like a head.

"This is the problem with bumpkins," I said. "Strength in numbers, but none otherwise. I'm just here to talk, Greer."

"Who the fuck are you? Marty send you?"

"If you don't know for sure, you're in a lot more trouble than you or your wife and kids think."

"Leave them out of it," Greer snarled. "This isn't about them."

"When you got in the business and started running it from home, it became about them," I said.

"What the fuck is that thing?" said one of Greer's mates, regarding the M10.

"A redneck grinder," I said. "It cuts trucks in two."

They only had the one shotgun among them, which surprised me. Greer's genius wasn't in city-style gangland violence but in training pilots willing to fly risky, treacherous missions in exchange for a lot of money and the ever-present adrenaline rush.

"Tell Marty I'm being squeezed," Greer said. "He's not the only one with a gun to my head."

Greer was sweating profusely, and it was only fifteen degrees Celsius. His band of nincompoops shuffled uneasily in the dirt driveway.

"I didn't pull this till I saw that," I said, indicating the shotgun. "My suggestion is to pick a side, or you'll be caught in the crossfire. Hint: you'd be wise to side with Marty."

"Have you met Chonen?" he asked, incredulous.

"Who's Chonen?"

"He's a guy who'd step on Mother Teresa's throat for a quarter. Makes Vincent seem like a party favor."

"I doubt that," I said. "Where is this imaginary Chonen?"

"He's been visiting Canada, acquiring associates."

"Associates. Everyone has associates," I said.

"He was dealing with Ng before Danny was shot. Now he's talking with Rio. You do not want to fuck with either of them. You tell Marty that I'll work for him if he protects me. No protection, no deal."

"Chonen about my height, white hair, green eyes?"

"You have seen him," Greer said, releasing a lungful of air.

Just as the situation was diffusing, Greer's idiotic wife exited the house with a .22 rifle.

"Everything's cool here, wifey," I said. "Get back in the house and tend to the kids."

"You won't get out alive if you fire that thing," she said calmly.

Kids or no kids, she was up to her eyeballs in this. What woman didn't like the dough-ray-me?

A couple of the boys behind Greer were bar brawlers with heavy rings on their fingers and not used to this kind of showdown. I was used to guns, and killing. Well, as used to it as you can ever get.

"The law of the jungle," one of them said.

"Tell Joe Rockhead there to put away the gun. Pull the trucks ahead and I'll drive out and give Marty your message. I've met Chonen. I can vouch for that."

The young men slowly piled into two of the trucks and pulled around and left the property. Greer stayed behind with one of his friends, a pudgy man with overalls and no shirt, his hands greasy. He had a ball cap with a helicopter on it and a logo I didn't recognize.

"I'll get working on Greta," he said to Greer and walked away toward the helicopter pad.

I slid the M10 into its holster and stepped around the car and opened the driver's door.

"I never wanted to get mixed up in all this shit," Greer said, looking honest enough. Looks can be deceiving. "The logging contracts are next to nil. I employ twelve people. I have a wife and four kids."

I didn't believe he was that naive. I knew for a fact he'd been involved with the Lone Wolves for at least six years. To have been smuggling across the border for that long without getting caught meant he was a sly fox. But standing in front of him, I could see from that distance his pulse inflating his overworked arteries. His face looked beat red, like it was about to explode.

"Hey, it's big money," I said. "It's big money, honey."

I stepped into the Skyline, put it into gear and pulled around his truck and went warily on my way, fully expecting to get ambushed by the bush league toughs in the other two pickups. The way was clear though, and as I sped down the gravel road, the dust billowed behind me like the vapor trail of a CF-18.

37

Manny Rio was a 6'2" Filipino man with a Spanish accent. He had an oblong head made tougher by a nose that had been broken so many times it looked like a mutant yam that had been mashed into his face. His nickname was "Cube," as in ice, which is where he typically put people when they got in his way.

Manny's girlfriend, Sumintra Mahdy, had the Bollywood features of an East Indian goddess. In my surveillance, I took several photos of her and marvelled at her face's perfect symmetry. Her smile sent shivers down my spine even through a telescopic sight at a hundred yards. Still, she didn't measure up to Ramona. Sumintra's constant sneer warned of a nasty individual.

Les Echevarria was Rio's second in command. He was a small, slight man with a moustache, who resembled the boxer Manny Pacquiao, so people called him Pacqui, which often was confused as Paki. Carl Bindha and Harrinda Sing were hitters who had cut their teeth in the Mumbai mafia run by Dahwood Ibrahim, the boss of what was arguably the world's largest organized criminal outfit. This meant Bindha and Harrinda were likely stone-cold killers, even though they didn't look like much. Bindha had a bald pate and a scraggly beard, and Harrinda was so skinny you might have been able to take him out with a 2H eraser. They had made it into Canada, though, with squeaky clean sheets, an accomplishment in itself.

They lived in Surrey, which always baffled me. Surrey was consistently voted the best-run city in Canada, yet for some reason, perhaps its geographic location, it housed much of Vancouver's criminal underworld.

Manny may have been the most successful of Vancouver's midtier operators, but he chose to live in a nondescript house on three acres in Cloverdale, a much smaller spread than any of the acreages owned by Lone Wolves but built on the same premise: distance between neighbors can only be a good thing.

Ethnic gangs in the lower mainland had begun as a way of sticking together to deal with racism and to aid each other in financial success, but they had become well oiled in less than twenty years. Violence is power, but in that, the Lone Wolves still had a monopoly— McViolence, Extortion-Mart. The Lone Wolves had the ability to call on other chapters, to bring in hitters and cleaners from outside their jurisdiction and to earn cash returning the favor. The Quebec chapter was their most ruthless.

After spending a few nights spying on Rio's minions, I headed over to Lonsdale for a little vitamin R. Ramona buzzed me up, so I was surprised when I found her in the middle of a session with Mia, and as I watched, I began to feel a little like an alcoholic who begins to realize he is poisoning himself.

Ramona had on jeans so tight they looked as though they had been e-coated on, and a pair of brown leather boots that hugged her calves and ended just below the knee. She wore an olive green tee shirt with a blood red Japanese symbol for peace, her exposed flexed triceps glistening with beads of sweat.

Mia was naked in the center of the bedroom, kneeling, arms spread out, her body warm and milky, surreal in the dim light. On her left ass cheek was a tattoo in script that read, *Ramona's*. There were no welts on her...yet.

Ramona stood behind Mia.

"How much did you bring me today?"

"Nine-fifty, madam."

"And yesterday?"

"Twelve hundred, madam."

"Are you happy with that, slave?"

"No, madam. It's never enough. I'm sorry." There was genuine angst in Mia's shaky voice, but her hips were gyrating ever so slightly.

Mia's accent mystified me.

"You're not sorry. You're lazy. You know, one of my clients complained about you, said you weren't into it. Do I need to remind you that when you fuck clients, my reputation is on the line?"

"Yes, madam, I'm sorry I've disappointed you."

"Quit saying that. You're not sorry. You're lazy."

"Yes, madam, I'm lazy. I'm sorry for being lazy."

Ramona smiled and shuffled her feet to position herself. The whip in her hand came down on Mia's back. Mia's
body jerked forward.

"NO FLINCHING!" Ramona yelled. "I told you, no
displays, no flinching, no moving, no moans and groans.
I know it fucking hurts. It's supposed to. I don't do this
for you to act. If you're going to act, do it with clients for
Christ's sake."

From that point on, Mia kept her arms out at her sides
and resisted moving at all while Ramona lashed out with
her whip, expertly timing the rhythm so that the beating
sounded like a heartbeat drum. Around Mia's neck was an
antique pendant, a purple blue amethyst teardrop set in
yellow gold. From the color, I knew the gem was old and
from a Russian mine. Slowly Mia's back and rump began
to redden and welt, and then turn purple and blue in a
marbling pattern.

Like a grasshopper turned locust, Ramona's physiology
changed before my eyes. As she whipped up a frenzy, the
power she had over Mia enveloped her whole being. Her
eyes seemed to liquefy, and even the smell of her unique
perfume and body odor intensified, becoming strangely
musky. Joy and lust painted her face. At one point, Ramona
stood behind Mia and twisted her blond hair in her fist and
stroked her back with a thin cane that whistled through the
air and nearly split my eardrum. The pain must have been
extraordinary, and Mia couldn't help but flinch.

Ramona's face tightened, as though she was considering admonishing Mia, but instead she stood in front of

her, held the whip and cane out to her and said, "Kiss them and thank me."

Mia complied, showing utter obeisance.

"Good girl," Ramona said, but her voice didn't sound at all accepting. "You weathered the beating well. I'm going to allow you to eat me…from behind."

Mia' s eyes widened with delight, but she didn't dare move yet.

Ramona threw the whip and cane onto the bed, unbuttoned her pants and pulled them down to her knees, and leaned forward over the bed, exposing herself for Mia to service.

"Crawl over, slave. And don't forget to be grateful. You never know when I may deny you these favors…forever."

With great effort and through obvious pain, Mia shuffled on her knees till she reached Ramona. She placed both hands on her mistress's hips and buried her face between Ramona's ass cheeks with an abandon normally reserved for a dying man's last meal. That's when I left.

I went to the living room, poured myself a stiff one, and stood by the sliding glass door, utterly befuddled, the wires in my brain so crossed I wasn't sure if I'd ever be able to think straight again. I finished my drink, and when I left, all I could hear was Ramona's orgiastic frenzy from her bedroom down the hall.

38

I needed to soak my head. When I got home, I ignored Ramona's calls to my cell phone and land line, suited up, and went down to the swimming pool in my building and swam about a hundred laps to rid my body of the buzzing energy. The water would normally have been too cold for me, but this night the water seemed to flush out all the horseshit floating around in my cranium.

I was alone in the pool area. After the workout, I floated in four feet of water to let it take the weight off my back, and then went over to the hot tub, which was cooler than I liked but soothing nonetheless.

The window looked out toward the Fraser, but it was dark outside, and all I could see was my own face in the reflected light, which was apt: time to face myself and how to proceed.

Careful planning and surveillance had allowed me to get away with X-ing O, but that kind of lady luck likely wouldn't last. Not these days. Single person Hollywood-style hits are just not practical. When the military carries out an assassination, they use whole squads of highly trained soldiers; however, military operations are different.

In order to carry out any kind of illegal entry or switch flip-ping, one had the entire world of technology against him. The CSIS will use fifty personnel to handle the surveillance of anything that could possibly interfere with an operation.

You couldn't be too careful. Closed-circuit televisions, or CCTs, can be sorted with algorithms to piece together crimes. Even the swimming pool and hot tub I was in now had a security camera recording my image to a remote hard drive. Banks, Tim Horton's, and even grocery stores all have cameras, some of them pointing toward the street. Police can canvas entire neighborhoods and sort through the videos and follow a vehicle or person to connect them to crimes.

In addition to this, cell phones can be located through triangulation. That could work in my favor, though. When and where I logged in to a computer could put me away from the scene of a crime. Even without the kind of cover-age London has, it is almost impossible to not have your picture taken, whether by a CCT or some asshole with a digital camera or cell phone.

A chill went through my spine while sitting in the hot tub when the thought came to mind of CSI teams and MEs who can lift fingerprints off plastic bags and tarps that have been wrapped around a body and buried for years, which is why I always wore gloves, or who have seen so many crime scenes they can tell when one is too clean to be realistic. Different lighting techniques can reveal the tini-est of bodily material that can yield DNA or links to your clothing.

The only kind of killing that had a chance of going undetected was total random murder, because any and all connection to a victim will be investigated.

Kicking the shit out of someone was one thing, committing crimes like smuggling and extortion in the name of digging for the CSIS was another. But hits are something even the CSIS and the CIA are not always legally allowed to do. Not that they don't do it when they have to, and not that there aren't factions within each organization that have the know-how to do it on their own, without sanction, usually with political motives.

The need in me to wipe from the face of the earth the kinds of fucked-up pieces of shit that overpopulated the planet overwhelmed me now, had become a compulsion that had made me its marionette. But it wouldn't do me any good to go to jail. Think, Char, think.

When I got back to my condo I ignored the new messages from Ramona, found my netbook and made entries to the effect that I was surprised O had been murdered and asking myself who could have done it. I figured notes like this, should Mahood get hold of my computer, might help cover my tracks.

The hot tub had made me sleepy. I thought about another snort but decided against it. In the morning, I was meeting with Marty and the honchos of the MP gang. I wanted to be well rested and lucid.

I thought I might dream about O, or Ng, or Marty, or Vincent and the bear claw he wore around his neck. I thought I might wake up encased in that baked clay oven in

Afghanistan, the smell of blood and semen and gunpowder in my nostrils forever. What I dreamt about was Ramona and how even with her unimaginable physical talent she overtook you with her mind. In the dream, she lay on a puffy white cloud while Mia and I ran tongues and lips over her welcoming, goose-pimpled body, remnants of her silvery laugh emanating from the center of my being.

At two in the morning I woke, bolt upright, to cold, sweat-soaked bedding.

"Adios, Afghan fuck face," I said aloud.

I leaned over, picked up my phone, and dialled Ramona. She picked up on the first ring and said, "Yes, you can come over," and then hung up.

I washed up and dressed, and as I put on my shirt, I felt like my thoughts were being remote controlled. So much for being rested for my meeting with Marty.

39

Kinky for Ramona meant straight-up missionary. At these times, a strange cloud enveloped her and veiled her eyes like a curtain, one that if drawn back exposed cruel, horrific truths that were best left hidden. Desire was like an electric current running through my body and even after an hour and a half, I couldn't rid myself of my lust for Ramona. Perhaps it was my own buried psyche that caused my reaction, or maybe it was Ramona's distance.

I wasn't the only one. Mia had fallen under a similar spell. I lay in the dark kissing Ramona's breasts long after she'd fallen asleep, marvelling at her taut, muscled body lying on top of the sheets stained with her sweat and cum. It was not love I was feeling but something entirely different. Thoughts came to my mind like water bubbling from a spring, desire imbuing it with varying degrees of heat. I felt an utter lack of control, like I had when on foot patrol in Afghanistan.

Mild panic set in, but I was able to subdue it by lying back and focusing on my breath as my chest heaved up and down. It was a sensation like sliding down an insane, snaking luge chute, not a pleasant image after last winter's Olympics.

I leaned up and looked past Ramona to the clock radio on her nightstand: four thirty. My meeting with Marty and the boys was scheduled for noon. If I was lucky, I could still get six hours sleep.

I woke at 10:09 a.m. again. Ramona was not in the room. I could smell her particular brand of shampoo, so I figured she'd already showered. I climbed out of bed, found the towel she'd left me, and lost myself under the pulsating nozzle for a good fifteen minutes, until I had massaged the weariness from my shoulder blades.

After I'd dried and dressed, I went out and found Ramona in her office, on the computer, wearing a navy satin robe with large oriental-looking birds on it.

"There's coffee in the kitchen," she said. "Get a mug and come here. I want to show you something."

I made my way to the kitchen and poured myself a cup and then stood behind Ramona and watched with awe as she performed her craft.

"See, what I do is I have a YouTube page set up to lure fucktards to my Web site. Once there, they get addicted to photos and more videos, which they can download. It's amazing how many losers will pay $19.99 for a video of a woman telling them they're worthless. Anyway, the links have spyware that infects their computers. The programs send me their keystrokes, and voila, I have passwords into their e-mail accounts where I harvest reams of personal data and account numbers and passwords for bank accounts. I'm draining one now," she said with a rhythm in her voice.

I tried to sound intrigued when, in actuality, I had a dozen emotions rippling over me.

"Where do you put the money?" I asked. "I mean, can't that be traced?"

"It has to be laundered, which costs half the take. Usually I don't drain a whole account, but this guy's been a dick, wasting my time. See, they're never going to go to the police. A lot of these guys are married, have kids. They don't want this shit out there. It's safer to siphon smaller amounts off a larger number of accounts. Sometimes I can't help myself though. An hour of my time and after the money's cleaned I'll have...let's see...$4,700, just out of this one account."

I wasn't sure what she was telling me. The problem gangsters of any ilk have are their untrustworthy associations, their inability to keep it zipped. Ramona obviously trusted me. Why? I couldn't say. It surprised me that she would trust any man. I'd figured that was why she had Mia serving her in her home rather than some skinny dude in leather panties.

I put my hands on her shoulders and massaged her neck, to reinforce in her that feeling of trust in me she had.

"What do you do with the data you get from e-mails?" I asked.

"Sell it, mostly, unless it's useful. A lot of these fucktards, and fucktardettes, are into fantasies of being extorted, so they have little recourse when they are extorted and..."

"And you're not worried you'll be traced to your computer?"

Ramona laughed hard at that, shook her head, and said, "I have, like, a hundred hijacked PCs out there. Everything is done through those. No. No way I can be traced. Plus, I have a few alarms that'll sound if ever there's a compromise. And plus plus, I have special software that keeps spyware from working on this computer, which I change regularly anyway. Another trick is to disconnect the computer from the Internet and root out any problems that way."

I wondered if the infection I'd facilitated for Mahood was working at all. I doubted it. I thought Mahood had said they were getting information, but he wouldn't tell me anything he didn't want to. She wasn't who they were after, and they'd let her get away with almost anything as long as they thought she'd lead them to better nabs.

"Look, babe, I gotta go. I have to meet Marty at noon," I said, leaning in and kissing Ramona on the cheek. It was like kissing a cadaver: Ramona was as icy as a medieval castle but with higher walls.

Ramona was entering yet another bank account and draining it dry too, euphoria overtaking her. That was her addiction.

"Greed is always a criminal's downfall," I said.

"Be thankful. This is my greatest aphrodisiac of all. It's what makes me want to fuck."

By the time I left, Ramona was done siphoning and was on a Web site for custom fashioned boots and was inputting her measurements for a pair of thigh-high leather and PVC boots that had four and a half inch heels and cost $800 US.

I wondered if my accounts had been gleaned on my cruise through Ramona's site.

Outside it was raining lightly, the sky an even sheet of purple grey. It was only eleven a.m., but it felt more like a late evening light. Just as I reached my car my cell phone rang. I got in the Skyline and answered it. Marty was on the other end.

"Change of plans, my friend," he said. "Meeting's at one, at Watts's property, where you kicked the shit out of Kerwin."

"Good. I haven't eaten yet."

"Yeah, and you have to drive all the way from Lonsdale."

"How'd you know I was up here?"

"When Ramona wants something, she gets it. You know that."

I hung up and pulled into an IHOP off the highway and had a plate of pumpkin pancakes with two huge dollops of whipped cream on top and a carafe of coffee and felt almost white afterward.

Watts's farmyard looked different in the daylight, more like a fortress. At night, the chain link fence and barbed wire had not been visible, but in the daytime, even hidden behind and in hedges, the fence made the place look like a concentration camp. The buildings were less farm, more factory.

In the drive sat an orange twenty-fifth anniversary edition Harley soft tail and a gorgeous chopper painted flat black with cherry red metallic flames. Next to the bikes was a nondescript gold Acura that belonged to Rio.

Past the garage and two other outbuildings, a hundred meters distant, three men sat in a gazebo sheltered from the drizzle. Manny Rio faced me and noticed me but sat tight-lipped. Marty's back was to me. Next to him, facing Rio, was Carl Bindha, a man whose physical presence was nothing but who did anything and everything Rio told him to do, usually from behind and without warning.

I walked silently across the lawn through a light fog that engulfed the countryside. Marty turned and saw me, and then turned back again to face Rio.

The gazebo was shaped like an octagon, and when I stepped up into it, all I could hear was the soft patter of rain on the cedar shake roof. None of the men looked at me, and none of them uttered a word. It was as if time had stopped, giving me time to think. Trying to decipher the confounding behavior of sociopaths like these three can take you in circles, so I didn't try. I could feel the weight of the Sig Mosquito inside my jacket holster. I saw no weapons with Marty or the MP members. I flexed the fingers on my right hand, like a western gunfighter about to draw. I figured it'd take me point two seconds to pull the gun and cap both, if need be.

40

"Have a seat," Marty said at last. His voice sounded hoarse, like you'd expect it to when you saw his bloated face with the three-day beard that looked more like black mold.

I sat, next to Rio, purposefully too close. I could feel him staring at the side of my head, but I didn't bother to look.

"Manny, Carl, this is Char," Marty said.

Rio cocked his hand toward me. I looked him in the eye, shook his hand, then leaned across and shook Bindha's.

No drinks, no snacks, no bullshit. A meeting on Lone Wolves' territory was a power play. Neutral turf implies equality.

"I was just telling Manny, here," Marty said to me, "that it's in his best interest to ixneh the arweh. We don't mind them all killing themselves, but think of the business."

Marty smirked at his perceived cleverness. But he was right. When wars or arrests thinned the talent pool, violence raised exponentially, a direct result of the power struggle in the vacuum. Prices rose too, and that benefitted the Lone Wolves, but overall Vincent Knight wanted an end to the gunplay. Many factors in the war, however, were out of his control.

"We deal with you. We deal with others," Manny said. "We don't step on your toes."

"We know you're dealing with Whitey," I said to Manny without looking at him. I decided picking lint off my pants would be a good visual. "The kind of goods he's bringing in and his goal to set up camp, that's bound to affect our relationship."

"Don't be sending that French fuck our way again," Manny told Marty. "I see him coming I'll plug the fucker."

"You won't see him coming," I said, not knowing who the French fucker was but able to guess Marc Glasner, "nor will you see me. Bottom line? You're small players. You have a bit part. You look big when you strut around the nightclubs impressing bimbos. Fuck with us…?" I feigned slitting my throat.

"Don't take it personally," Marty said. "It's business. There's moola for everyone. Just don't forget the pecking order here. Be happy with what you've got."

I actually couldn't believe it needed to be said, but the fact was that the Lone Wolves needed gangs like the Tarantulas and the MPs and even the gutter balls to bring their product to market. True, there would always be someone on the streets, but no business liked having its staff decimated, whether by the pig flu or gang war. But when you read the papers or watched the news, it was always the gangs like the Tarantulas and the MPs shooting each other: you rarely heard mention of the Lone Wolves.

"I don't like the tone here," Bindha said in perfect English. His scraggly beard looked oily, his shaved head lopsided and moronic.

"Shut the fuck up," Manny told him.

Bindha swallowed his anger and looked away.

"Look out, Marty. The fucker probably has a bomb strapped to him," I said.

Bindha's eyes were unblinking and lidless, like a reptile's. He stared at me and said in monotone under his breath, "I'm a fucking Canadian, like you, asshole."

"You're nothing like me, you greasy piece of shit," I said calmly.

Marty had the look of a father who had just witnessed his son score the winning goal for Team Canada.

"The lesson here, boys, is that we've been sitting watching the bullshit going on, and we've just about had it," Marty said.

Bindha's eyes widened as I reached in my jacket, to pull out a pack of gum. I took out a square of Double-Bubble, popped it in my mouth, and threw the wrapper and cartoon to the ground.

Bindha stared at it solemnly, head down. None of these fuckers liked being told what to do. That was precisely why they found themselves in their line of work: they could never have had a boss man in a regular job humiliate them. The fear of violence and mountains of money kept them in line in gang life. The survivors, the ones who stayed out of prison, were the ones who kept a lid on it.

I studied Bindha's face carefully. There were no laugh lines, not even the hint of a smile line. Here was a kid whose probable brutal upbringing and lack of education made him unpredictable and dangerous. I refrained from saying anything and waited for Marty to talk.

"Look, boys, we're finished here. This horseshit keeps up, you'll have a full-metal suppository."

"You're talking with Ng, I hope," Manny said.

"Do I look stupid?" Marty said. "You worry about your end. Let me worry about them. Hear?"

Manny nodded and stood, indicating for Bindha to leave with him. The two men walked off without looking back, their shoulders hunched to the mottled sky that seemed to weigh down on the city.

41

When Manny Rio and Carl Bindha had gone, Marty shrugged his shoulders, shook his head, and made a face as if he'd just swallowed a rotten egg. Then his flip phone rang, his personal ringtone a wolf howling, which was apt. He looked at me while he spoke into the cell phone.

"Yeah. Mm hmm. No. No. I don't know. Good. No, they're gone. Well. He's still here. Yeah. Okay. I'll let him know. All right. Later."

Marty closed his cell and slid it into his jacket pocket and said, "Vincent wants you on call. The slightest problem with these fucks and you're up. You won't be the only one up, so you know."

"All right," I said. "You know where to reach me. Are we done here?"

He looked me over carefully, like a mechanic would look at an engine problem he couldn't quite solve, and nodded.

"You okay?" he asked.

"Not much sleep last night."

Marty nodded and sat with his hands on his lap.

"See ya," I said.

I got up and stepped off the gazebo. The wet grass soaked my shoes and the drizzle misted my bristly hair.

"Watch out for Ramona," Marty said, calling after me. I thought he meant protect her, but then he added, "She's a man-eater."

When I got to the privacy of my car, I called Mahood.

"What's the matter?" Mahood asked, like he gave a shit.

"I'm feeling wigged-out," I told him. "The lines are getting fuzzy."

Mahood was silent on the other end, contemplating.

"I'll meet you at the Keg, down from your condo, in an hour," he said finally.

As much experience as I had, I was a still rookie at this. On top of that, I was damaged goods. PTSD isn't just a description. It was dangerous for me to assume I was in control. Basic training ensured that. Unfortunately, on-the-job training was the best and maybe the only way to tackle infiltration.

I started the Skyline and put it into gear. Driving seemed to clear my mind.

The Keg was in what had been a railway station and was made of red and brown brick. It was quiet when I got there. Mahood was already seated. He wore a blue rainproof jacket that made him look like a policeman. I expected CSIS or RCMP to be written across his back in gold letters, but it wasn't. I ordered a steak sandwich and a glass of wine. Mahood decided on rib eye and an iced tea.

"Pressure getting to you?" Mahood asked.

I looked out the tinted windows toward the street. I could hear a train shunting nearby.

"You getting anything from Ramona's computer?"

Mahood looked at me suspiciously and answered, "We were, but it stopped. She's very clever." He offered nothing more than that.

I didn't want to spill my guts to Mahood, who was after all a cop of sorts, but I needed to talk to someone.

"I have serious concerns about what we're doing," I said, choosing my words with care. "This war on drugs is bullshit."

Mahood's eyes widened.

"The only way to keep drugs off the streets and out of the hands of kids is law enforcement," he said dogmatically. "You want…"

"Out of the hands of kids?" I questioned. "How well is that working? You can get anything, any time. Making it illegal brings the Knights and the Smukers and the Roos into the mix. These lowlifes will make money any way they can. The easiest fucking place to get smack is in prison."

A waitress wearing a tight black knitted dress and three-inch heels brought our food. While she placed the plates in front of us, my eyes gravitated to her bare, silky calves that flexed as she moved. She left as quickly as she came, my eyes on her rump. Mahood took his chance.

"The only thing keeping drugs in check is law enforcement. Imagine the free-for-all if drugs were legalized."

"Portugal legalized pot, and they have the lowest usage in the EU," I shot back. "This fucked-up right-wing agenda is based entirely on fanatical ideology. They hate science, which proves criminalization is fucking stupid."

"I'm not sure how you can say that," Mahood countered. "I've been on the streets, was undercover RCMP for eight years. I know what goes on down there."

"Do you? Treating drug use as criminal rather than a health issue is bananas."

"Bananas?" Mahood said, laughing.

"Look, these fuckers are into prostitution, gambling, extortion, you name it. They'll put their mitts into anything black market. As soon as you ban something people want, someone will supply it. Did prohibition work? Criminalizing pot, a six billion dollar a year industry in B.C. alone, gives huge cash flow for other operations."

"It'll never get legalized," Mahood said flatly. "Not in our lifetime."

"Not with the US of fucking A across the border. The fundamentalists there are rewriting textbooks to brainwash kids and live their whole lives oblivious to what's in front of their faces."

"Who cares what the US does?" Mahood offered.

"The further to the right they go, the further we'll go."

"Well, we disagree on this. Look, if you're so…"

"Listen, man, I put in my time in Afghanistan. You CSIS dudes look more and more like the CIA every day. A poor man's CIA."

Mahood grimaced, and for a millisecond resembled a toothless old man.

"You saying you can't do your job?"

"I got nothing else," I said. "You know it, I know it. That's the problem. That's most people's problem. Look, these fuckers are dirty to the bone, and there are enough reasons for me to be putting the toe of my shoe up their asses. But you, Vulture, and everyone else at the top needs to see the light. Harper is the most myopic fuck I've ever seen. He probably thinks dinosaur bones were put there by God to fool us."

"Just focus on what you need to in order to get the job done. Fact is, Xy is trafficking workers, women, weapons, *and* drugs. As you say, there are lots of reasons to cancel his ticket and to put a monkey wrench in the Lone Wolves' operations. And don't make the same mistake most good-niks make: think of yourself, your life, your need for an income. No one else will."

That was true. I sawed off a chunk of steak and gnawed on that for a while. It was refreshing not to hear my diatribe. Like most therapy, I was answering my own questions.

"There's enough wrong out there that we can all pick our battles," Mahood said, pointing at me with his fork. "Just don't bite off more than you can chew."

I nodded as I gulped down my wine, resisting the urge to say anything more.

"And another thing. We may disagree on some points, but I respect you, Char. If you want to change things, get into politics. And we have a job to do. We have many common goals. Let's focus on those."

Mahood was saying things I agreed with, but his job, among other things, was to stand me up and brush me off.

"All right," I said. "I feel better having vented."

"Good," he said, his face relaxing. "Hey, guys like us, we need to stick together. No one else understands what we do, what we see. Why do you think I've been divorced twice? And who likes everything about his job?"

Mahood ordered a coffee, and I ordered a double Jack, neat, and waited impatiently for that.

"And think of all the things you like about the job," Mahood said convincingly. "Where else could you boot-fuck like you do and get paid for it?"

He was right about that. The waitress brought my drink and set it down and paused while looking directly into my eyes.

"Will that be all?"

"Yes. Just the check," I said.

She left the table, and with a perfunctory gesture, she returned and left the check at my sleeve. I picked it up and turned it over. On it she'd left her name, Angel, and beside that a phone number, hers I assumed. I looked over at her near the cash register. Her eye caught mine momentarily, and then in a fit of embarrassment, she stepped into the kitchen.

"Feeling better, I see," Mahood commented.

On our way out the door, Mahood turned up the lapels on his jacket, but the rain had stopped. The pavement was oily and slick and nearly took the feet from under me. We went our separate ways, Mahood disappearing around the corner. When I reached my car, I couldn't help but feel something was wrong. It was the same eerie sense

I'd gotten in Afghanistan just before sniper fire. My commander had told me that in WWII snipers documented victims looking down the sightline: they sensed their watcher even from hundreds of yards. I stood by my car and spun on my heels, looking around for whatever had its beady eye on me. Nothing. It was several minutes before I pulled on the handle to get in the Skyline.

42

Three whole days had passed since my meetings with Marty and Mahood, without a bleat from anyone. It was the first three-day stretch for me in a while. I tried calling Ramona, but she wasn't home and wasn't returning my voice mails. I drove by her building just before dinner one night, but the lights were off in her unit, and I saw no sign of her. I decided to regard it as a good thing.

I thought about calling Angel but declined for now when I realized my urge to call her was rooted entirely in my need to have Ramona.

I went to a matinee after training for two hours. Sitting in the dark by myself emptied my mind of extraneous thoughts, if temporarily. I exited the theater in Coquitlam feeling clear-headed, fit, and pain free—three things that had not come together for me with that congruity since before the war. It should have been the first warning. The smile reflected in my rearview mirror should have been the second.

Many Afghan vets, PTSD sufferers or not, have a difficult time integrating back into the regular world. Not that the regular world isn't rife with its own horrors, but the constant feeling you're being hunted when not in a war zone is irrational and something my work didn't help diminish. But that was why I liked the work. I thought it would mesh well with a psyche that was forever fucked. I never wanted to distrust the sensation that electrified my entire being, though, causing me to tuck in my chin and hunch my shoulders like a K-1 kickboxer.

The odd impression followed me as I drove through traffic. I could almost see my entire body and car covered with crosshairs.

"If someone really wants you dead," I said aloud, "you're dead. There's nothing you can do."

I decided to park away from my building. I rummaged though the glove box and found a small can of bear spray and put that in my pocket. I had no gun with me in the car, so that would have to do. In the trunk I found a Seahawk's ball cap and tugged that down over my head.

The street was quiet, the sidewalk bone dry. I approached my building and entered through a rear door, looking down to avoid the camera mounted up in the corner. I took the back stairs to my floor and peered cautiously down the hallway: no one. I thought about my neighbors, tried to remember when they were usually home. The unit across the hall was likely empty till Ms. Clairmont came home after six. I glanced at my watch. It was five thirty-five. I crept over the carpet and pressed my ear to my door and listened. I heard nothing.

Silently I inserted my key and rotated it as slowly as I could. At the end of the turn, there was a slight, metallic clunk that I could feel in my fingers but not hear. I opened the door in one, smooth motion, the bear spray levelled at my hip. In front of me, in the hallway leading to the living room, looking like a moose caught in the headlights, was a man my height, thickly muscled and bald as a cue ball, wearing jeans and a sallow wife-beater muscle shirt, both arms sleeved in tattoos, some raw prison tatts, others impeccably drafted. But before he'd turned to face me, I'd seen the one that mattered. Arced across his upper back, partially hidden by the material of the wife-beater, were the words *Lone Wolves*.

"Bonjour," he said, smiling. Then he laughed, a laugh that sounded like an emphysema victim drowning.

He bared small, pointy teeth, which made me think of how a barracuda would look if it smiled. He still hadn't noticed the bear spray at my hip.

I doused him from ten feet away. If you've never seen a man hit with pepper spray meant to bring down a thousand-pound animal, you don't want to. The man who'd sold it to me on Vancouver Island told me you feel like your insides are turning out, and vomit accordingly.

I closed the door. 'Cuda was thrashing now and kicking my nice walls, so I hoofed him one in the ribs, and that seemed to quieten him. Thankfully the units were soundproof. I figured if anyone else was with 'Cuda they'd have shown themselves. After twenty minutes, he managed to get to his hands and knees.

"Can you hear me, 'Cuda?"

"Wha?" he said, his mouth hanging open, spit drooling to the hardwood floor.

"This is ending here. You leave, tell Vincent you had a chat with me, I'll say I got the message, and you won't have to deal with me again. Understand?"

He heard me but was in no frame of mind to process it. I went through the kitchen and into the living room through the other entrance. 'Cuda's patched coat and 9mm Beretta were on the loveseat. He must have gone to the kitchen and was on his way back when I came in. The TV was stationed at the front foyer camera. He hadn't seen me come in, wasn't expecting me. I brought the man a glass of water, set it down in front of him, and backed off before taking a quick look throughout, making sure no one else was there.

This was Vincent Knight's way of letting me know not to get too confident. It had probably been a mistake to cut down Kermit at the soiree at Watts's. What's done is done, I thought.

'Cuda made it to his knees, wiping puke from his chin and looking like he'd swallowed a gallon of slop water.

Now, when you get knocked out, you lose five minutes or more of your life. Seeing 'Cuda kneeling in front of me was as far back in my mind as I could go. When I woke up, my living room had been trashed, and two uniformed policemen were standing over me, the static on their radios clamping my head like a vice. I lay propped against the wall with remnants of my flat screen scattered around me. The neighbor from across the hall, Ms. Clairmont, was in the doorframe, looking concerned. She was an actuarial assistant in her midfifties. She had her hands on her hips like she was the one in charge.

"I chased him out, officers," she said.

"Did you get a good look?" one of them asked.

"Oh, I got a good whiff, all right."

The room spun counterclockwise, and it was my turn to lose my cookies. My knee was throbbing, and I could feel blood dribbling down my left cheek.

I tried standing but couldn't.

"Take it easy," one of the uniforms said. "Paramedics'll be here in a minute."

I tried mumbling something.

"What was that?" the cop asked.

"He said, 'Cuda's good. Real good,'" Ms. Clairmont said.

"Who the hell's 'Cuda?" he asked.

"The guy who did this," she said, annoyed. "Do I have to do everything for you?"

Without any resistance from me, I let the paramedics hoist me onto a gurney and wheel me out to the ambulance. A little observation couldn't hurt. I tried to thank Ms. Clairmont, but all I could manage was to lift my hand, like I was hailing a cab.

43

I stayed in Royal Columbia overnight, on a gurney in a hall off the emergency room. I'd taken a beating but had given one too. My knees and elbows were sore, and my right hand was swollen across all four knuckles. But you don't wake up if you've won. My left eye was swollen half closed, and I had a hematoma the size and shape of a golf ball over my left temple. My ribcage felt like a halftrack had driven over it, and I felt nauseous and had a headache that could have killed a river horse. I sat on the edge of the bed having to admit to myself I may have owed my life to a spinster.

When I left midmorning, I was cursed with the thoughts any fighter has after taking one on the chin. I tried never to take losses of any kind personally. People with no losses on their records aren't fighting the best; they're padding their fights. I liked testing myself, and in a street fight anything can happen. Also, there was always time for payback. Unfortunately for me I hadn't a clue what had happened, what, if anything, I'd done wrong, or what 'Cuda had in his tool kit. Maybe I'd ask Ms. Clairmont. Maybe I wouldn't.

The first thing I did was phone a maid service and explain to them what I needed, and then spent two hours with them while they cleaned up the debris and vomit in my living room and hallway. It wasn't so bad, really. I needed a new TV and end table. A few ornaments I couldn't have given a shit about were busted, but I'd find replacements in the antique market below. Everything was tidied and lemon scented by the time the maids left.

Vincent Knight, the orchestrator of my recent grief, had committed unconscionable acts of violence and crime rising up the ranks. I didn't have the evidence for this, but it had to be true. He wasn't far from the age many people retire at, and here he was, pulling the strings of a multibillion-dollar criminal empire, living in beautiful homes, driving half-million dollar cars and never paying for it except in the form of the torturous thoughts that had molded and contorted his face over the years.

I rented a car and staked out his Horseshoe Bay home, which was built like a fortress. There was no way onto the property without climbing a ten-foot high fence, and who knew what was on the other side? His primary residence was in Belcarra, past Port Moody on the far side of the inlet, and was similarly guarded. I also followed him to the Watts property, three times in two days. A lot of gangsters seemed to drift to the eastern side of the Greater Vancouver area. Compared with downtown, it was Sleepy Hollow.

I thought carefully while sitting in the rental car down the block from Vincent's Belcarra mansion, a massive timber-framed, log affair barely visible through the trees between it and the road. I had little recourse that would keep me from eating one of their bullets, should I ever take my feelings to the Lone Wolves. No matter how tough I thought I was, there were just too many of them and way too much money. Money can buy a lot of trouble. There didn't appear to be a way for me to hit them without eventually getting smoked.

In my mind, I saw a Predator, the remote-controlled US attack plane used in Afghanistan to hit insurgents over rough terrain and in impenetrable compounds. I didn't have a plane, but I had something even better, something I would need to prep for if and when the time came. This inspiration brought a smile to my face. I looked at myself in the rearview mirror and patted the swelling.

"Thanks, 'Cuda. There's nothing like a loss to get you mental for the big show."

After I dropped off the rental I got in my own car, bought myself a new TV, and headed to the antique market where I bought a new table and a few glass ornaments to compliment my decor.

On the way home, a headline in *The Sun* caught my attention. I bought the rag and took it home with me, and after getting a syringe and draining blood from the hematoma, I sat down in my kitchen, poured myself a cup of coffee, and read:

Vancouver: A man was murdered execution style yesterday in White Rock. Ted Westbury was found by neighbors in the driveway outside his home.

"He was such a nice guy," a neighbor who wished to remain unidentified said. "Quiet, friendly, helpful. He was always helping people."

"This looks like a gangland slaying," IHIT spokeswoman Lise Cruz said. "We're still investigating. The victim has no known criminal associations as far as we know."

So I had been right. Ted the welding truck driver did have death written across his forehead. I read the next piece:

Vancouver: A Surrey woman was gunned down today as she drove her daughter to day care. Sumintra Mahdy was driving south on 176th when a vehicle passing in the opposite direction fired over the cement meridian and riddled her vehicle. The nine-year-old girl was not injured. Sumintra Mahdy was the wife of Manny Rio, known leader of the MP gang based in Surrey.

Integrated Homicide Investigative Team spokesman Tim McClure told reporters this was a targeted hit and that citizens need not worry about their safety in that regard.

"My concern," Tim McClure said, "is that these gangsters have no concern for innocent bystanders or even children."

When asked about the spate of unsolved gangland killings in Vancouver recently, McClure responded by saying, "These investigations are incredibly complex. We can not go to the Crown with scanty evidence."

A group of about twenty people protested outside Surrey City Hall, urging authorities to put an end to the violence.

The article was accompanied by a photograph of a blue Porsche Cayenne SUV halfway in a ditch, the driver's door left open, a woman slumped forward on the steering wheel. Behind the vehicle stood a fence and an old mare grazing in a farmer's field.

These murders were my perfect cover.

44

Two days later, with sunglasses on, I didn't look worse for wear. Marty had called late the previous night to give me the coordinates for my next muscle job. His voice was guarded, like he expected me to tell him to fuck off. 'Cuda wasn't something to discuss, though. I'd pissed off Vincent. Everyone would piss off Vincent at some junction. He hadn't got to where he was by not being a violent control freak. Not Vincent, Marty, Marc, or any of these douche bags were the communicative type. You didn't express your feelings to them, especially if you wanted to keep your cards close to your chest, or your chest for that matter.

It interested me that the Tarantulas had murdered Rio's wife. I had no proof, of course, but since it wasn't me, it had to be them. The majority of this shit wasn't a mystery to police. What was hard was proving it in a world rooted in silence and deception. Snitching was a way to make yourself a dead man walking. The murder was a bold, if idiotic, statement. It said that they were willing to do whatever it took, but also that they had not been able to get to Rio himself, who did seem smarter than Lyle Ng. The MP gang was, by definition of their membership, harder to spot. All the Tarantulas were oriental. The only thing you could say about the MP gang was that no one was white.

The job given to me was to find and reign in two hookers the Lone Wolves sold off Craigslist, Mercedes and Scarlett. I knew those weren't their real names. To the Lone Wolves, they didn't have real names, didn't need them. The women in question were working in Langley out of a motel, and rumor had it that a new gang out of Abbotsford called the Snakeyes had attempted to take control of prostitution in that area. These were young men in their early twenties who didn't know any better, so my job was to school them.

I met Marty in the parking lot of Willowbrook shopping center, off the Fraser Highway. The name Willowbrook made me laugh. Developers have a way of bulldozing natural landmarks and then naming the development after whatever has been paved over. There were no willows here, and no brook, just acres and acres of asphalt.

I sat in Marty's Tundra while he handed me photos of the two girls. Mercedes was blonde and skinny and pregnant in the photo, Scarlett was mulatto and defiant in her eyes, but the skin that sagged on her postpubescent face said otherwise. These girls, runaways usually from abuse and violence in the home, were no match for the brutality of the pimps associated with the gangs. Although the two girls couldn't have looked more different, both faces had the identical look of hopelessness. My heart sank.

I took the photos and tucked them in my Caballero pocket while glaring out the window without saying anything. For the first time, I really had to control my anger toward Marty. It's easy to forget when hanging around these assholes while sharing a drink or a joke that someone on the street is carrying out their horror.

"What's the matter?" Marty asked.

I had my glasses on, but you could still see the goose egg.

"What's that, Mr. Sunshine? You're always in a good mood?"

"You seem out of sorts," he said.

Marty had on jeans and a jean jacket, a kind of fashion crime that outstripped his other vices. I almost told him I didn't want anything to do with the girls, but decided there was no need to share that with him. He showed me grainy photos of the two Snakeye members he wanted me to "talk" with. These were white guys, rednecks to the hilt, more so than the dunderheads I'd visited in Merritt.

"This one is Clay Moore," he said, tapping a picture of a man bloated with muscles. Moore had no neck and wore a Punishment Athletics tee and had several gold chains around his neck: perfect for strangling him with. "This guy is Andrew Weybourne."

Weybourne was less muscled but also an obsessive lifter.

"I like the lifters," I said. "Slow, physically and mentally."

Marty said, "They have Snakeye script tatts on the inside of their wrists."

He turned his own wrist and rubbed it, and from my seat, I could see the pale white line of a scar there where either he or someone had cut him. The stitch marks made the scar look like a centipede.

He told me their normal hangout and said, "Kick the living shit out of them, Char. Give it to them good. Something to remember. Find the girls and call me. Stay with them till I get there."

How I felt right then as I stared at Marty through my sunglasses was exactly how I felt when I couldn't shit, like I had a grenade up my ass.

Superimposed now over Marty's face was the Afghan pedophile, staring at me, his beard trembling, a beard supposed to mean adherence to his religion. At least Marty didn't go to such ends to disguise who he was. He wore it on his back, in the form of a tattoo and a fucking patch sewn onto his stinking jacket.

Fear ran though me like coolant through a big block. That was good. Fear heightened my senses, but flashing before me now, along with the Afghan's face over Marty's, was the realization of how murder sprees can happen: the real source of anger and hatred overlaid onto other people.

I left Marty's truck and headed for the Skyline. The air was dry and the sky a powdery grey blue, sunshine bouncing off the bottoms of the leaves as the wind blew, but all I could see was the Afghan pedophile and his accomplices. All I could smell was semen and gun smoke; all I could feel even in that cool breeze was the baking heat in the clay room cooking my innards.

Coolant or not, I was a boiling and ready to blow.

45

After three days scouting, I tracked the steroid freaks to a dingy motel in Langley. Langley is east of Surrey, not far from the Fraser, a community that is part of Metro Van and a push-up away from twenty-five thousand people. It is also the home of the Cruise In car show every September, which I hoped to attend this year. But for now, my attention was on Bodily Fluids Motel, which sat as a relic from the 50s in a relatively new semi-industrial park. Few trees surrounded the L-shaped stucco building, which looked as though it had recently had an exterior spray job. Cheap, mildewed aluminum windows accented the cream colored stucco.

"They couldn't plant one tree?" I asked myself as I sat in my car in the lot of an industrial strip mall facing the motel, where my ride was lost amongst the sea of cars.

Swinging the toe of my boot into the pelvic bone of every myopic recidivist east of the Pecos gave me a warm, cozy sensation. I sipped my Tim Horton's coffee after spending a lifetime trying to secure the flap on my cup, wondering, "Why the hell they don't use sippy lids?"

Clay Moore and Andrew Weybourne pulled into the motel parking lot and nosed the silver Infinity SUV in front of unit 14.

"Party time," I said.

I put the cup in the holder and reached into the glove box and found a pair of fingerless driving gloves, put those on, picked up the ram's head ring, and slide it on to my fuck-you finger and tucked a telescopic police baton into my jacket next to the Sig Mosquito and stepped out of the Skyline.

Clay's and Andrew's day was about to take a drastic turn. I looked both ways as I walked through the lot. I was far enough away from the sign-in office so that if they had a camera it couldn't see me from there. I saw none on the outside of the building. The curtains of unit 14 were closed. I walked past the Infinity and to the door. I almost busted #14 down but decided for some reason to try the knob. Why they left it unlocked was uncertain. Maybe they weren't staying long—only long enough to collect the money. I walked straight in and opened and closed the door.

Both men were so surprised it was as if they were wearing nothing but cement boots. Andrew was closest to me. He had on a Do or Die hoodie with an octagon cage chain-link pattern on it. In one fluid motion, I withdrew the baton, and as I swung it, the unit elongated and came down on the base of his neck just as he started to say, "What the f…?'

He went straight down.

Clay was six feet away with a chair between us, in which Mercedes sat.

"Fucking cocksucker," he yelled while lunging at me with his right hand cocked, but having the speed of a semi loaded with old growth. I patterned his face with the ram's head, dropping him, too.

Mercedes yelped, and then Scarlett came out of the washroom and screamed too.

"Shut the fuck up!" I yelled. "Get in the can."

Both gaping jaws slammed shut.

Andrew was hurt bad. He rolled on the floor at my feet clutching his neck. Controlling a man's head and neck was always a good tactic, says Pop. Clay jumped up though, faster than he had lunged at me but, as intimidating as he looked, all he had was strength. His fists were up at man-boob level. I roundhouse kicked him on the temple, and he fell sideways onto the bed and thumped onto the carpet and rolled next to the chest of drawers.

I scanned the room for weapons but didn't see any.

Mercedes stepped back, and she and Scarlett shuffled into the bathroom. I leaned over Andrew and, grabbing his hoodie, rolled him over to face me.

"Andrew, my friend. Know who I am?"

He shook his head while crooking his neck to one side and managed to garble, "The Purolator man?"

"That's pretty fucking funny," I said, laughing. "I'm an employment councillor, here to tell you that you need another line of work."

With one eye on Clay, I knelt on Andrew's chest and threw three rights, stamping his face with the seal of the ram. Blood spurted from the wound over the bridge of his nose.

Clay was dazed but getting up again. He said, "Jesus fuck, man, what's your problem?"

He was looking for something to hit me with. He grabbed the table lamp, but it was bolted to the table.

I booted him square in the nuts, dropping him again.

"Strike three, you're out," I said.

Clay managed to get to his knees. At least he wasn't a quitter, but that was going to get him killed. I put my foot between his shoulder blades, stomped him back down, and then brought the baton down on his ass a half dozen times. Even with jeans, it made him thrash. I waited a few seconds, rolled him over, and squatted down to him and spat on his face.

"You know what you are?" I asked rhetorically. "You're way, way out of your fucking league. Fuck with us again and it won't be this fun. Now get your friend up, get in the expensive car your mom bought for you, and drive the fuck out and don't come back. I see you anywhere, anytime, I'm gonna pull your plug. Understand?"

He nodded with is eyes closed.

"Say it," I told him.

"I…I understand."

"Understand what?"

"To leave, not come back."

"And leave the girls alone. Read my lips. Not your property. Understand?"

"Yeah," he said with spittle on his lips. "Not my property."

I patted him down and withdrew from his pants pocket a roll of bills and stuck it in my own pants. I let Clay up and backed toward the washroom. The girls had the door closed. I got a good look at the room. It wasn't bad, although I knew what motel rooms looked like under infrared lighting. Clay shook Andrew and pulled him up and stood with him, glancing back at me and hesitating at the door. Meatheads like that can't stand losing, but they have no idea what it is to really lose.

"Clay!" I said. I had put the baton back in the pocket and pulled from its holster the Mosquito. "Just in case you're packing in the truck and think you're smart."

He glanced down at the handgun, shook his head, opened the door to the rest of a day he'd rue for a long time, and left. I went to the window and peered out a crack and saw the Infinity back up and drive off, Clay yelling at Andrew and pounding the dashboard.

When I was sure they'd gone, I went to the bathroom door and opened it. The girls were clutching each other in the shower, the curtain pulled.

"Get out, now," I ordered.

I got out the roll of bills and counted it in front of them.

"Twenty-four-eighty," I said. "That's twelve-forty each." I counted it off and handed each her share.

The girls stood wide-eyed, mouths puckered and unable to speak. I knew their story. They weren't prostitutes; they were slaves, being held and forced into tricks and given only enough food and clothes to keep them alive.

"I'm taking a big chance here. Leave town, now. Go east, anywhere, out of B.C. Don't come back. I see you, I'll take care of you, hear?"

Mercedes nodded.

"You didn't see me. You snuck out the window here. Pack, now, and get out. Call a cab from Tim Horton's. AM I CLEAR?"

"Y-yes. T-thanks," Scarlett said, her voice shrill and childlike.

I took off the ring and flushed it down the toilet, then washed my hands in the sink, and wiped my hands and the taps with the towel and kept it with me when I left, held it under my coat as I made my way to the car, my head turning side to side like a tank turret, expecting anything and everything to come my way.

I made it to the Skyline and got in and started it, buzzed down the window, put it into gear, and released the clutch.

A woman in a Sunfire passed me, her window cracked, Van Morrison's signature voice singing: "…I'm a working man in my prime…"

46

It had been a week since I'd seen Ramona. She called me finally, just as my balls had turned the appropriate shade of blue.

"Where've you been?" I asked, my voice quavering. "I've been trying to get hold of you."

"I can tell," she said, her laugh short and condescending. "Seven messages. Missing me?"

"With every bullet so far," I shot back.

I was on Lonsdale within the hour, feeling a bit like a racehorse gaining speed around the final turn. What I found wasn't at all what I expected.

Ramona was pale and withdrawn, even if she was as beautiful as always. She wore a black, skin-tight track suit with a tan bead of trim down the sides of the sleeves and pants. She wore a pair of brand new running shoes. Here she was living in a beautiful condo, money coming out her ass, any kind of sex a crooked finger away, and she was depressed and unhappy. I didn't delude myself that I wanted to or even could change that. What was wrong with Ramona went through her like rot in wood.

She got me a lowball filled with Jack and held one her-self and drank from it as if it held her savior. It didn't. She swallowed without blinking.

Her pallor was like a blanket over her soul, making her more distant and cold, if that were possible. Her ginor-mous tits reminded me of Jessica Rabbit's. In her mood, I had no confidence making a move even though that was why I was there.

Something else was off.

Without a word to me, Ramona moved toward the balcony, slid the glass door open, and stepped outside. She leaned against the railing, and I left her there alone for a moment and then followed her out.

"Anything you want to talk about?" I asked, sidling up to her so that my shoulder touched hers.

"No, why?" she said, her voice cracking, betraying her words.

I let that drift with the breeze.

I sipped my whiskey. Ramona gulped hers down and looked at the empty glass as though it were a lover who had jilted her.

Without cause or warning, Ramona laughed a laugh that had the metallic lilt of Satan's door chime. I looked at her but didn't bother to ask. Ramona set down her glass, took my hand, and led me to the bedroom and took off her warm-up suit to reveal a lovely red thong and match-ing bra that had to have had coat hanger wire in it to hold up her breasts, her body breathtakingly surreal in the soft light. Her touch was not warm like that of a lover and oddly withdrawn. But it was her eyes that told the tale. Her eyes glowed, alternating between red and white hot, like an ember in a dying fire.

"Take your clothes off and kneel," she commanded.

"What?"

"You heard me, Char. Take off your clothes and kneel. NOW!"

"Listen," I said. "I don't mind playing games, fantasizing in the middle of it all, but I'm not Mia."

The look on her face should have been reserved for witnessing a jetliner flying into a skyscraper at the speed of sound. She slapped me. I grabbed her wrist. She tried kneeing me and elbowing me, and I had to remember that she'd trained in MMA for years, that in spite of her 118 pound frame she knew what she was doing. I grabbed her under her arms and, twisting her upper body away from her feet, tossed her on her bed and watched her bounce.

"What the fuck are you doing?" she said furiously.

She jumped up but on the other side of the bed.

"Save that shit for your slaves. You're insane if you can't separate them from me."

Ramona was breathing fast now, her chest heaving. Her remarkable beauty was disarming, but I knew I could never trust a psyche that was peppered with bombs like a dirt road in Kandahar. I'd been burnt by that before.

Ramona burst into tears, but I was in no mood to hold or comfort her.

"Fuck off. Get out," she said curtly.

I stood utterly motionless.

"GET OUT! NOW!"

"That I can obey," I said at last.

She picked up a glass ornament shaped like a bunch of grapes and tossed it at my head, narrowly missing. It put a chunk out of the wall's paint job but miraculously didn't break itself when it skidded across the floor.

I spun on my heels and split the joint. I wasn't upset. Horny yes, upset? No. By the time I got outside, I had my shit together enough to remember not to walk under her balcony. Who knew what she'd throw from there? She was a disaster that could befall some other schmuck.

That didn't stop me from doing something dangerous. I went on a bender, losing a battle with a bottle of Cazadores, but at least I had the brains to do it in my own home, with the lights off and without answering the phone, which rang at least ten times. It was Ramona calling, but I wasn't going there. Not now, not ever. So I told myself. I was smart enough to know that desperate desire didn't work that way.

I tried not to think about Ramona, her moist lips, her smooth, unblemished skin, her flawless breasts, her McIntosh apple ass, or the euphoria I felt in her having me, and I tried my best not to talk to myself. That night, when I finally fell asleep, I slept the sleep of the dead.

47

I woke at ten in the morning feeling surprisingly good. Ever since I stopped mixing my drinks, hangovers had become a thing of the past. I had drunk two large glasses of water before crashing, and felt like a new man, but decided to keep the old one.

After a plate of bacon and eggs-over-tough and three chunks of sourdough toast all washed down with thick coffee, the phone rang. The call display indicated Marty. I swallowed hard and picked up.

"Hey, Marty. How's it?"

There was an awkward pause, and then his somber voice saying, "Not bad. Could be better. Where's Mercedes and Scarlett?"

He was breathing heavily.

"They made it out the bathroom window. Sorry, man. My fault. I told them to go in there while I was dealing with the meatheads."

My story sounded plausible, but I doubted the timber of my own shaky voice. I had busted out the bathroom window before leaving the motel room, to make my story plausible, but because they are rats themselves, guys like Vincent and Marty know a rat when they smell one.

"Mm, hmm."

"Look, Marty, things don't always go as planned. The Snakeyes or brown eyes or whatever they're fucking called will think twice before making another move. No unfinished business there."

"Hold on a sec," Marty said, his voice an actor's lesson in disappointment.

I heard shuffling in the background and was certain I heard Vincent's voice. The phone went dead.

"Fuck you too," I said as I turned off my phone. I hadn't set the goddamned thing down yet when it rang again. I nearly chucked it through the window, but when I looked at the caller ID, I saw it was Mahood.

I was too angry to say hello.

"You there?" Mahood said.

"Yeah, I'm fucking here."

"Who shit on your cornflakes?"

"Marty."

"Oh," he said, resigned. "Listen, IHIT wants to talk to you. Ronald Watts's Langley property was raided for weapons charges after a neighbor witnessed a man wielding an automatic rifle. What they found is a bloody slaughterhouse. They haven't even begun to determine who has been murdered or where the body or bodies are."

"Why am I not surprised?" I asked myself out loud. "Look, once these fuckers get a taste of doing what they want, whenever they want, there's no limit to their debauchery."

"This is beyond debauchery, my friend," said Mahood. "Anyway, I informed IHIT Detective Ford you may be of some help. I doubt anyone associated with Watts'll talk."

"I'm not a fan of this, Mahood. My cover is my life. That fuck-up VPD detective who tried jacking me at the River Rock is symptomatic."

"We've been dropping a noose around him and his partner. Not as widespread as you'd think, just some bad eggs. Listen, cops aren't all good. I'll be the first to tell you that. Take my word we're aware of that angle. And I've told Ford the interview is between you and him only. I'll be there with you."

"He knows I'm on the up and up?"

"As much as he can. Look, these guys don't trust us any more than city cops in the States trust the FBI or CIA."

"Jesus Christ," I said.

"What?"

"I've been on that property a few times. Lone Wolves are there all the time. I followed Knight around for a few days, and he was on that place like a fat chick on a box of Laura Secord's."

Mahood noisily cleared his throat.

"When's this Ford guy want to see me?"

"I'll let you know. In the meantime, stay away from the Lone Wolves."

"Marty's miffed at me. I had a muscle job the other day and let two young prostitutes go. I was supposed to bring them to him. He suspects I'm a softy."

"Like I said, stay away for a bit. Get sick. Tell him a relative is in town. Anything. Just keep them at arm's length for now, just a day or three."

"All right. Thanks."

"You'll be hearing from us."

When I hung up, I went to the window with my cup of coffee and stared out over the churning grey waters of the Fraser, which looked clean enough until a rusted barrel did a summersault momentarily on the surface, or a giant tractor tire drifted by, looking at first like a circular shadow. The one cloud in the sky blocked the sun's light like a bandage on an open wound. I finished my coffee and went for a walk.

My legs took me to the antique market where I found myself amidst a room of bric-a-brac. My mind temporarily forgot whatever horrors waited for me at the Watts's farm. Inside a glass case, my eyes caught a beautiful 1950s lighter shaped like a Doberman's head.

Two days later I read the newspaper story on Watts:

Vancouver: On Tuesday at five in the morning, Integrated Homicide Investigative Team members cordoned off a property in Langley Township owned by Ronald Watts. Spokesman Lem Ford told reporters they are investigating at least one murder, in addition to several weapons violations.

The thirty-acre Watts farm is part of a block of land purchased by Watts's parents, Johan and Emily, in 1957. Upon the death of Emily in 1982, Ronald Watts and his brother, Lincoln, sold parcels for a reported fifteen million dollars. Lincoln took his half and moved to Nanaimo. In addition to his share of the cash for the land, Ronald kept and lived in the original homestead, which has several outbuildings, including a brick structure that had been converted into a private party lounge.

Ronald Watts is a known associate of the Lone Wolves, and members of the notorious biker gang are often seen visiting Watts and attending parties there. It is not known precisely what role Watts has with the gang, which controls the drug and prostitution trade in the Lower mainland. Mr. Watts has been taken in for questioning.

Late Tuesday a dozen CSU vehicles and a mobile command center were driven onto the property. Early Wednesday an excavator was brought on site. IHIT spokesman Lem Ford had no further comment.

48

Three days after I read the first article, the scope of the horror began leaking out. Parts of at least five separate bodies were found in a freezer in the veranda of Watts's main home, under boxes containing free-range bison meat. At least Watts was careful about what he ate. Bone fragments were being sifted from every corner of the main compound. IHIT had no idea who the victims were or where they'd come from.

Thankfully Mahood accompanied me to the meeting with Detective Ford. He picked me up in a blacked-out Escalade and sat in the back with me as a stoic driver drove us to the Watts farm where we exited the vehicle directly next to a forty-foot motor home that served as an office for the detectives. We trampled over a couple of feet of dried, uneven mud and went up the metal steps and in without knocking.

Inside, the trailer smelled like alcohol hand sanitizer and wet metal. Lem Ford was alone and wore a dark brown suit with a light blue windowpane pattern on it. He stood to shake my hand. He was an inch taller than I and was breaching fifty, his wrinkled, puffy face and his loose chicken-skin neck belying his wide shoulders and narrow waist. He was the best dressed cop I'd ever seen.

"Mr. Sadao, I'm Detective Ford. Please have a seat," he said, gesturing to a comfortable chair adjacent to his desk.

"Thanks," I said, taking his offer. My legs felt weak, my head light.

Mahood sat down in the chair beside me.

"Do you prefer to be called Charles?" Ford asked.

"Char's fine. It's what everyone calls me."

"Short form of Charles?"

"No. I was burnt in a vehicle rollover in Afghanistan," I told him, getting out the information that I served my country.

He nodded while looking down at his desk at an enormous amount of paperwork, all neatly arranged in piles that he moved about like a shell game till he was satisfied.

"Down to cases," he said, looking at Mahood and then me. "What can you tell us about what you've seen here that might help us?"

That was a broad question.

I shrugged, shook my head, and said, "I've been here a few times. Once was a party for the Lone Wolves. About a hundred members, associates, and their girlfriends were there. It was held mainly outdoors but in the brick building as well. I purposefully beat the living shit out of one of the Lone Wolves' enforcers, to send a message. I paid for it later," I said, indicating the discoloration that still surrounded the eye. "Spent a day in hospital after Knight sent a hitter to my place."

I cleared my throat nervously while Ford looked into my eyes, waiting. His were rusty, the mottled color of iron. He looked detached, which you'd have to be in his shoes.

"On another occasion, I came here to meet with Marty Smuker and two members of the MPs, who had been getting out of line," I went on. "That day Marty also gave the orders for another job, a muscle job in Langley."

"At the motel?" he asked calmly.

I nodded. These guys were fucking good. I began to question my actual role.

"I spent a couple days following Vincent Knight, to get a bead on him. He came here like a porn addict to the Internet. His chopper was here the day I met Marty, but I didn't see him. I only ever saw Watts the night of the party. The place always gave me the heebie-jeebies."

"And you haven't been here other than that?"

His voice was accusatory, but I knew that I hadn't been there other than the times mentioned.

I shook my head while he sat back in his chair, his hands folded behind his head, staring daggers into my eyes. He picked up a folder and held it guardedly in his hands. Outside I could hear voices and then a man barking a command. Someone knocked on the door of the motor home.

"Not now," Ford yelled.

Then, with glacial speed, Ford leaned forward and handed me the file folder and said, "I'm sorry to have to ask you this. Please look in the file, to the photos there. Tell me if you recognize her at all from your dealings with the Lone Wolves and Ronald Watts."

I rested the file folder on my lap and opened it as if a boxing glove was going to pop up and punch me in the snout. Inside were two photos of a dead woman's body, front and back. I looked at the frontal shot first. Bits of soil had not been brushed off. Somehow the skin looked surprisingly soft and touchable, but I knew the clammy sensation of death. The woman's scalp and face had been removed, almost entirely. A small tuft of her hair brushed her left ear. There were no earrings or jewellery on her fingers. A chunk of skin had been cut from her left and right arm.

I looked at the photo of her backside. Her entire back was covered with lash marks and cigarette burns. On her right cheek, where it had said *Ramona's,* the skin had been removed entirely.

I clambered for sanity, keeping my eyes down on the photos long enough to gather my thoughts.

"You know her," Ford said.

"I'm thinking," I said. "I don't see shit like this every day. There were a lot of people at the party. I'm trying to go back in my mind."

After a few moments, Ford said to Mahood, "We need Char back in there. No one will talk, least of all Watts. If he does, it'll be his death sentence."

We all knew this wasn't just Watts. We all knew that since it was his home, his property, he would pay. But what had really gone on? Who were the real perpetrators? My mind drew to visions of Vincent spending an inordinate amount of time there over the last while. Whoever it was, I knew he would never see the inside of a cell.

I closed the file folder and tossed it on the desk in front of Ford and said, "I'll keep my brain working overtime. And I agree: I should be back in the mix. They might get more suspicious if I bug out."

"*More* suspicious?" Ford asked.

I explained to him about the prostitutes.

"Keep me posted though your normal chain," Ford said, nodding toward Mahood.

I stood unhurriedly, my legs and back feeling stiff and sore. Mahood got up, extended his hand, and shook Ford's.

"Thanks for not showing me the photos," Mahood said.

Ford and I hesitated but shook hands at last, and I said, "I don't envy your job."

"Right back at you, son."

As we left the motor home cum office and stumbled over the rock-hard dried mud and back into the Escalade, my thoughts went to Pop. I vowed to call him within the week. Maybe he could anchor me.

The sight of the farm bloated with CSU vehicles and personnel seemed distant and surreal through the smoked glass.

"There's no end to the depths people will sink," Mahood said in an uncharacteristic moment of despair.

There was nothing I could add to that, nothing at all.

49

Marty called the day after my meeting with Ford. "Saturday we need you in Belcarra. You'll be security with a number of other members and associates. There'll be some men at the gate. The password is *Oyster*. Be there by one."

Marty hung up the phone without pleasantries. He was distancing himself from me, but I needn't try to dissect that. Men like Marty are so complex in their fucked-up-edness that it was better left alone.

These orders were simple enough. Friday night I had a training session and avoided drink of any kind. I woke early on Saturday, stretched, drank a protein power shake, and put on my nicest Caballero bulletproof suit, a silver one with an exquisite cut, chose a pastel orange tie to go with it, and admired myself in the long mirror. I headed to Port Moody around ten o'clock, to make sure I got to Vincent Knight's on time if I got held up by traffic. I sat outside a Starbucks, next to the Skyline, sipping on my Americano and getting a kick out of the women admiring the suit. I looked like Sexyama. At twelve thirty, I got in my car and drove to the boss man's estate.

The men at the gate were full-patch members who wore suits today, their mutt faces sticking out from the Armani suits off-putting, like seeing a codger wearing a spinner hat and tight jeans. The one who came up to me had long, frizzy hair and wore the scars of a long lost battle with acne. His oversized mandible hardly moved when he spoke, like he had a toothache. His raspy voice was as incongruous to his suit as his face.

"Password?" he asked.

"Cunt."

"Good enough," he said, waving me through.

He'd never make it in my army, I thought.

I drove up past the log manse, which had a carved sign above the main entrance: Valhalla. It was a massive log structure, unlike any I'd seen. I parked out back amidst fifty choppers right out of a show 'n shine and a collection of cars cut and pasted out of the Dupont Registry, including Knight's Phantom, two Audi G8s, an Aston Martin Vantage, and a beautiful gull-winged Mercedes with a matte, gun-metal finish. I patted the Skyline.

I was staring at the sea of chrome when Marty's voice carried over from the rear of the house.

"Over here, Char."

I strode over to where Marty stood and looked up at him on the deck. Massive timbers framed the structure.

"C'mon up," he said. "I'll show you your post."

I found the stairs and made my way up toward Marty's ever-changing moods, which kept me off-balance, Marty's intent.

Marty also wore a suit, grey with thin pinstripes, his gut testing the stitching, his round face, soaked in a lifetime of drinking, smoking, and partying, looked pale and uninviting next to the cloth, and his teeth looked yellow and uneven. It's like when you paint your living room only to discover that now your carpet looks terrible, so you change that, and then your drapes suck.

"There's an important meeting here at two. I want you inside, next to the great room. What're you packing?"

I showed him the M10.

"Jeezus," he said, flinching.

"There's more, but I'll keep it to myself in case you turn on me."

I smiled with that last comment, but Marty, who had glanced out the window, watching another car come into the back lot, cocked his head in my direction and studied my face.

Right back at ya, fuck-head, I thought.

"Take a stroll around, see where everything is. The great room's toward that wing," he said, pointing to my right and then slapping my shoulder like a buddy would. "I have to head out back."

I took that stroll around. Valhalla was no log cabin. It had to have been ten thousand square feet. Each room could have fit two condos like mine, including the shitters, and Vincent actually had an impressive library. The feature walls were log, but other walls were drywall and covered with fine, impasto paintings, which was obviously Knight's preference.

In the front room, there was a massive French lime-stone fireplace that on close inspection seemed to be carved out of one, solid piece. It was twelve feet high, eight feet wide at least, with the slightest tint of yellow marbled in its opaqueness. Doors decorated with bull's eye glass separated most of the rooms. L'Ouiseau's Westmount mansion in Montreal had nothing on this place. The irony of both L'Ouiseau and Knight living on the opposite ends of the country and of every other scale I could imagine brought a goofy smile to my face. I had no doubt Knight was by far the wealthier of the two and had gained his wealth not only from the degree of his psychopathy, but from the so-called war on drugs, which handed the bikers a near monopoly in this corner of the continent.

A meeting like this had to have been scheduled long before the Watts farm had been invaded by police, but it was obvious when I saw Knight, resplendent in a black European suit and standing with his wife, Jessica, a statu-esque strawberry blonde who looked like she'd be right at home on any red carpet, that he didn't have a worry on his mind. He pulled out a globular chromium lighter, lit a wooden pipe, and then pointed the pipe in my direction and winked at me. Just then a huge paw engulfed my shoulder. I turned to see who it was.

Mini-me towered over me, looking down and smiling like a Cheshire cat. He wore slacks and a sports jacket that could have tarped Knight's Phantom. Under the jacket, he wore a faded tee.

"How's it going, my man?" he said, ramming a croissant into his gullet.

I brushed crumbs off his lapels and said, "It could always be better, little guy."

He reached around him, picked up a mug, and drank from that. I could smell the coffee.

"Where'd you get that?" I asked.

"What, the good looks?"

I pointed to the coffee.

"I'll need to show you."

The house was a maze. Mini-me led me through two corridors and past at least seventeen rooms. Along one wall, outside of what I realized was the great room, was a row of urns and food, ranging from candied salmon to Nanaimo bars and fruit.

I helped myself to a cup of Java and stood in the entrance to the great room. In it was an ancient table made of planks and a stained glass ceiling depicting what looked to me to be a Viking scene, through which natural light streamed. Spaced carefully and spotlighted along the walls were more carvings and impasto paintings, one of an ancient vessel plying the North Sea. There were no windows in the room. It reminded me of a state room on a yacht.

"This is my posting," I said to Mini-me. I asked him, "Where'd the name Mini-me come from?"

"My dad," he said, stuffing Nanaimo bar into his mouth and washing it down with more coffee. "We look alike, but he's really big."

He was looking very serious. He wasn't kidding.

I didn't see Kermit, which was good, nor the French fuck who'd broke in to my condo. I figured Ramona wouldn't be there either, unless I grossly misjudged her role. This was strictly business.

"Know what the meeting's about?" I asked Mini-me.

"Yeah," he said, nonchalantly.

"Well."

At that instant, Whitey walked in from the back and went straight toward the great room with nary a glance. He wore a gorgeous white suit and tie, which made him look like the man from Glad or like the leader of an alien cult. I decided not to call him that, here at least. The man he was with, though, had not accompanied him to Tofino when I'd met Whitey for the exchange. He was Chinese and had severe features and wore an olive green suit and a red tie, which made him look like a general from the Revolutionary Army. When he saw me, he stopped in his tracks, halting Whitey, but waited till he was inside the great room to whisper into his ear.

"Dong Kim Il there noticed you look like Xy," Mini-me said.

So that's what this was about: a business agreement between Xy and the Lone Wolves. It made sense. Perhaps Xy's men had been searching for the right partnership, stirring the pot to see what rose to the top. Or maybe it was a matter of "if you can't beat 'em, join 'em."

I felt discomfort standing there, but after contemplation decided I didn't mind being a grunt for Vincent Knight

and his hooligans because that's not what I was in reality. After they all piled into the great room and the doors
closed behind them, the rest of us stuck to our posts, patting our weapons from time to time, glancing at the retinue
of bodyguards Whitey had brought with him. These were
four small oriental men, all dressed in similar dark green
suits and all of them with facial scars and nervous tics that
caused them to twitch. Cheap, hired violence. They kept
near but avoided eye contact, even with each other. Two
spoke Cantonese.

I didn't see how anyone here could be protected. If a
gun battle broke out, I decided I'd just dive out the fucking
window, bullet-proof suit and all. So many bullets would
be flying in that scenario not even my Caballero suit would
stop shrapnel from slamming into my face. I could teach
these morons a lot about proper security, but I wouldn't.

After two hours of complete and utter boredom on
what was looking to be the warmest day of the year, the
great room cleared out, and everyone funnelled into the
front room, where a bartender handed out drinks in highball glasses that looked like they'd been chiselled out of a
glacier tongue. I was on duty and couldn't drink, which
was fine. I stood next to Mini-me, marveling at Jessica's
dress from behind, careful to not ogle.

How did the VPD not know about this meeting? That
was the beauty of the code. Then again, maybe they did.
Vincent lit his pipe again and, with his wife under his
arm, led Whitey and a few other guests around the room,
explaining the paintings. All seemed cordial. After enjoying

a few drinks each, Whitey and his Chinese partner left satisfied and in the end jovial, along with their impassive bodyguards.

I made a trip to the back and looked out the window, noted the two identical blacked out Mercedes sedans, and went to one of the washrooms where I texted Mahood this information. After that, I rejoined Mini-me.

Marty came up to me and Mini-me and said, "We're having a little do here. You guys are welcome to stay and have a drink or two."

That sounded like a good idea to us. We made our way to the bar where I ordered a double Gentleman Jack and Mini-me ordered Alberta Premium.

"Best whiskey, period," Mini-me said, holding up his glass. "America can fuck itself."

We left the bar area to allow others up and stood by one of the halls leading to the private area of the home.

The swelling in my loins came first. Mini-me tapped me on the shoulder, and I looked up at him. He pointed toward the far end of the hallway behind me, and I turned to look.

Ramona stood staring at me, hands on hips, her weight shifting to one leg, a petulant look on her lips. She wore black knee-high boots and ribbed leggings, and a black top that flawlessly framed her unimaginable symmetry. Michelangelo couldn't have carved a better looking woman.

"It's Ramona," he said, as if I didn't know.

I did the only thing I could have done. Like a chunk of scrap metal drawn to a magnet, I strode over to Ramona, cupped her face in my hands, and kissed her as fully and deeply and passionately as I'd ever thought of kissing anyone. She smelled like Chanel #5 and cum mixed together. She kissed me back, running her tongue along mine and pressing the palm of her hand to my groin. Then she pushed me away from her and laughed coldly, sounding like shards of ice tinkling in a thawing northern lake.

"So fucking easy," she said.

She held my hand in her vicelike grip and led me up the stairs to one of the seven bedrooms, where she made love to me as only Ramona could.

50

I t's my way or the highway," Ramona said.

I was already naked, my limbs strapped to each of the four twisted posts of the plantation bed, when Ramona began to striptease above me, taking care to dig the heels of her boots into my nipples before she unzipped them and tossed them aside.

"Kiss and lick them," she said, standing on my stomach with one foot while pressing the other to my face.

I gladly ran my tongue the length of her soles. The taste of leather mixed with Ramona's own flavors caused me to swoon. I licked and sucked the soles of Ramona's feet as though I'd never tasted anything before, which brought delight and color to the surface of her skin.

"If you don't like it now, you will," she said, basking. She suddenly withdrew her foot from my face, peered into my eyes, and said, "Oh, you want more?" Then she laughed.

I had seen Ramona several times naked, but when she took off the rest of her clothes, I couldn't believe any woman could be so physically faultless, the tautness of her tan skin and muscled physique directly out of an anime.

"You'll lick what I say, when I say, suck what I want, when I want, hear me?" she whispered while fitting me with a condom. "Even cock." She looked back at the door to make sure it was still locked. "It's not just me you're obsessed with," she said. "It's your own fucking desires. Haven't you figured that out yet? There's no escape from those. Ultimately, I'm replaceable, but your desires are there for good. Now, do *not* cum till I say."

Ramona mounted me while facing away at first, then spun to watch me, or mock me, because when she was finished cumming for the first time she rose up, her stomach heaving with joy, then sat on my face, her ass cheeks spread, her anus above me.

"Know how to French kiss a Greek?" she asked, laughing at her wit.

My tongue and mouth were there before her sentence was finished.

"Good boy," she cooed. "Lots of patience, no pride. That's it. Ah, yes, like that. Deeper. Now rim me."

She was adamant I not cum and knew if she even breathed on me I would, so she rolled off the bed and stood next to it, hands on hips again and smiling at me triumphantly.

With a shrug she dressed, did her hair, refreshed her makeup in the adjoining washroom, came back in the bedroom, and sat in an armchair and addressed me while I lay bound and in the midst of the most gruelling pleasure I'd ever felt.

"You'll crawl on broken glass to get to me," she said melodically, "especially if I tell you to. All I want to hear from you from now on is, 'Yes, Ramona.' 'Right away, Ramona.' 'How hard Ramona?' Do you understand, Char?"

All I could manage was a weak nod.

"Say it, Char. Say, 'Yes, Ramona, I'm yours. I'll do whatever you say, when you say it, however you tell me to.' Say it, Char. You know you feel it."

I repeated her mantra, though much more slowly than she had said it. Exultant, Ramona stood, walked across the carpet to me, and began undoing the straps that held me to the bed. I was still lying, exhausted and excited to the point that my lower extremities were pulsating with each heartbeat, when she placed her index finger between my lips and, fucking my mouth with it, said, "Know what you need, Char? You need a tattoo, right on your ass, one that says, *Ramona's*."

She left the room without me, saying, "Don't wash your face before leaving. Use it to think of me. And fix the sheets before you go."

Slowly I dressed myself and checked my reflection in the mirror. I smoothed the sheets on the bed and wiped water from around the sink. I checked my wallet. Ramona had drained it of the three hundred and change that had been in there. She didn't need the money. It was some kind of kick she got out of that.

When I came down the stairs, Mini-me met me by the food tables, put his arm around me, and walked me outside.

"I feel sorry for you, man."

He was being sarcastic and hadn't the slightest clue who or what Ramona was. Then again, Mini-me had surprised me before. "See ya later, Char," he said as he walked to his Suburban.

The Skyline had been baking in the sun. Feeling utterly drained, I started it and turned on the air-conditioning but stood outside of it while it cooled off. Next to the garage, I could see a flash of yellow. I stood over to the side to see what it was. It was Ramona's Hummer. I stood motionless for a moment, wondering what to do. I decided to stroll over. As I got close, I could see that the rear hatch was up and that the vehicle's suspension was rocking slightly. I went around back of it and looked straight into the Hummer.

The Klingon that had been on gate detail was behind Ramona, who was still clothed but had her leggings down and was on all fours, and he was plunging himself deep inside her. At first, he was too busy to notice me. Ramona looked behind her and locked eyes with mine, her expression changeless.

"Go away, fucktard," she snarled. "I'm done with you for today."

Worf looked back. He didn't seem to mind me being there.

"Go away," she insisted. "Or next time I'll reverse the order."

I stepped away and back to my car and sped noiselessly out of Vincent's drive. After I'd gotten away from Valhalla, I stopped the car and stared out over the arm of Burrard Inlet, catching my breath. I cranked the rearview mirror to face me. Looking into the depths of my own soul, I couldn't help but see: it wasn't Vincent, it wasn't Ramona, and it wasn't anyone or anything else.

The vision that stuck in my mind wasn't Ramona on top of me in Valhalla, nor the Klingon fucking her in the Hummer. What impressed itself into my mind like a boot print in shit was the vision of a half dozen chains hanging from the dashboard of the Hummer, one a purple/blue amethyst teardrop set in gold. All four tires smoked when I left the curb and catapulted home.

51

The following week Watts was charged with the murder of five unknown women.

IHIT spokesman Lem Ford said in a television interview, "We currently are gathering evidence. It may be months before we are satisfied with our search of the property. We are sifting through a mountain of calls from the public, most of which is unsubstantiated or completely false. I'd like to take this time to tell the public that giving false leads is extremely damaging to a case. We need to pursue these leads, and any time we spend on bad information keeps us from doing our job."

There was absolutely no news about the Lone Wolves, either in the Watts case or in the gang wars that were invading Metro Vancouver's streets. The layers of insulation kept the Lone Wolves organization far removed from police investigations. Not that members weren't nabbed from time to time, and not that they were immune from being shot at or beaten in street fights. However, Lone Wolves were strangely absent from any form of justice I would want to see.

It's true, too, that the Lone Wolves run the port in Vancouver, though perhaps not to the degree they once did. Their tentacles reach deep into the unions that run the facility. How does that make the port authority feel, especially when questions of security arise? Most ships bound for North America from Asia are cleared in ports there, ports that are rife with corruption. The likelihood of even a suitcase nuclear weapon landing on North American soil in this manner was, in my mind, extremely plausible. I brought this up with Mahood, who dutifully made a note in his little scribbler before tucking it into his shirt pocket, like he gave a shit.

Careful to not be followed, I headed to Steveston to train with Pop. I'd never be able to forgive myself if anything ever happened to Pop because of me and my work. On this day of training, Pop strained to instil in me the notion of movement, combinations, and how to transition from karate to pure boxing and back again, to confront your opponent. He stressed feints, deception, striking at a distance. Each style had its strengths, and even though he was a karate man, he saw the usefulness of blending.

The catch wrestling we worked on focussed on stand-up clinches and how to dirty box. Even the best strikers clinch when they're in trouble. What do they do then? Pop taught me a new toss, which relied on neck and shoulder control. When someone controls your neck and head, you go where they tell you to go.

There was fire in Pop's eyes. He's always emphasized the finishing game. He liked to spend hours on the details of ending the fight, whether by fist, knee, shin, elbow, choke, or limb separation and fracture. I once saw an old film of Pop fighting in Northern California in the sixties, when he nearly tore the arm off a judoka who wouldn't tap.

"If you're too proud to know when you've been beaten, too proud to take your hat off to a man who's beaten you, you're too self-centred to ever learn from your mistakes," he'd say.

I knew better than to doubt Pop. As good a fighter as he was, he was a better talker. I remember as a teen coming across a road rage incident. Pop left our station wagon wearing confidence like a badge. He stood between two men who brandished tire irons and in five minutes had become their friend.

He didn't tell me how he felt about me so much as show it in the light in his eyes when I listened to his training regimens. I think he wanted me to fight professionally, thought it was an avenue for me, a man who'd survived a war in a desert on the other side of the planet. He'd never mentioned it, though, and any tension he may have felt was alleviated with the work I did now, even though he didn't actually know what that was. At last I had some dough.

After training, we decided to go to the river for a bite to eat. We sat in the Shady Island Seafood Bar and Grill, looking at the sheet of dark water move in one piece toward the strait. A tug powered along, toting a small barge with a faded orange pile driver on it. The sun shone low through a metallic dome of sky and, as the day wore on, illuminated only its own form in an otherwise darkening sky.

A tall, svelte blonde in flats, black slacks, and a white blouse brought our sparkling juices to the table. I ordered the king crab leg meal, and Pop had the Cajun halibut wrap while flipping through *The Sun*, which sat next to his sweating glass held in his right hand. His high cheekbones and militaristic air meant he could never be mistaken for a Chinese, Vietnamese, or any other nationality, unlike me, who could be mistaken for every race except white or black.

"Listen to this," he said while following the line with his index finger. He read me this article:

Vancouver: In the wake of escalating gang violence in Metro Vancouver, a high-ranking member of the LoneWolves has been targeted. Vincent Knight, president of the motorcycle gang for the last twelve years, was at his Belcarra home Wednesday when he received a package containing a single antique lighter.

"He collects them," his wife Jessica said through tears. "This one looked like a Doberman's head. After he unpacked it, he handed it to me. I lit it and then handed it back to him. I'd just stepped away when it blew up in his face."

Vincent Knight was taken to hospital where he is in intensive care and listed as critical.

In another incident police say may be related, Ramona Roos, Knight's niece and a known associate of the LoneWolves, was found dead in her North Vancouver condominium. She apparently died of cyanide poisoning after she, too, received a gift from the post, this one a bottle of Flowerbomb Extreme fragrance by Viktor & Rolf laced with cyanide. Roos was twenty-seven.

"What in hell can you make of this?" Pop asked, incredulous, patting the newspaper with his left hand. "I mean, what is the world coming to?"

I had no answer for him. Hell, I had none for myself. I just played the cards dealt me.

52

Vincent Knight died one week later.

"Good fucking riddance."

I had no delusions about the Lone Wolves. Someone would take Knight's place, maybe someone even more ruthless and violent. The gang had survived worse. My only regret was that I hadn't hit 'Cuda. But I took Pop's advice to heart. What's in one loss? Anyway, I had no doubt I'd run into him some day soon.

A cursory search on the Internet found dozens of women similar to Ramona, maybe not as tied to organized crime and theft as she, but dozens nonetheless. I knew from the Pickton case several years ago, where Willy was convicted but not before admitting he was low on the totem, that neither Knight nor Ramona would even get questioned, and I'd have to live with the vision of Mia's ravaged body overlaid onto the Afghan pedophiles that were a regular stage play in my mindscape.

I reclined on my balcony puffing on a Punch and sipping some of the Premium Mini-me had sold me on. I had three drinks already in me, and my hand was still shaking, which it was wont to do.

Halfway through the cigar, I poured myself another stiff one, hardly feeling the liquor at all as it flowed down my throat and into my veins, the booze beading and rolling off my conscience. That's when my phone rang at my side.

"Char, how are your nerves holding up?" Mahood asked.

"Not bad," I said. "Nothing twenty-six ounces of therapy can't fix."

Mahood paused, probably wondering how serious I was with that comment. Not too serious, I could have told him, but I was caring less what anyone thought about me.

"We think we have a lead on the Watts girl," Mahood told me in a conciliatory manner.

"Go on. I'm listening."

"Her dental work was consistent with Eastern European countries. We've done a facial reconstruction and think we've traced her to Macedonia. We think she was smuggled here and used in the prostitution trade. We think they're trading women back and forth. One informant remembers seeing someone who looked like Mia in a strip club in Delta." He paused for a second and added, "We have some good leads anyway."

I may have gotten Scarlett and Mercedes, or whatever their real names were, out just in time.

"McRape," I said. "Thanks for telling me."

"Any hunches on Knight's murder?" he asked.

I hesitated, stumbled over a syllable or two, and managed to say, "Only that whoever did it knew what the fuck they were doing. Unfortunately nothing will come of it. Nothing ever does."

"Can you stick it out?" Mahood asked. "We're close to Xy. Your slot with the Wolves might give us our break."

I said yes after realizing he couldn't hear my nodding.

Xy was just one tumor in the cancer, like Knight: excise the growth and another one comes along, perhaps a genetically mutated one for which our remedies don't work.

"Good. Look, get some rest. Hey, heard from Marty?"

"Mmm, no. Other things on his mind, I suppose."

Mahood laughed a loud HA and hung up. I set down my phone, adjusted my reclined position, and took a long pull on the Punch and a tug on the Premium, which tasted like liquid gold. Across the Fraser, framed by industrial blight, a dinged aluminum fishing boat struggled to land a sturgeon half again as long as the men on the boat. Not far from the boat a huge, baby blue tank of some sort, streaked with oil and covered in Chinese letters, drifted on past. You just never knew what would rise to the surface.

With cigar and drink in hand, I began to shake with laughter, or maybe tears, or maybe an indistinguishable mixture of both. Either way, I couldn't stop it for the longest time.

Made in the USA
Charleston, SC
01 November 2011